WATCHERS IN DEATH

THE BEAST ARISES

Discover the latest books in this multi-volume series at
blacklibrary.com

THE BEAST ARISES

BOOK NINE

WATCHERS IN DEATH

DAVID ANNANDALE

BLACK LIBRARY

For Margaux, and to her voice.

A BLACK LIBRARY PUBLICATION

First published in Great Britain in 2016 by
Black Library
Games Workshop Ltd
Willow Road
Nottingham NG7 2WS UK

10 9 8 7 6 5 4 3 2 1

Cover art by Víctor Manuel Leza Moreno.

See Black Library on the internet at

blacklibrary.com

Find out more about Games Workshop
and the world of Warhammer 40,000 at

games-workshop.com

Printed and bound in China

Fire sputters...
The shame of our deaths
and our heresies is done. They are
behind us, like wretched phantoms. This
is a new age, a strong age, an age of Imperium.
Despite our losses, despite the fallen sons, despite the
eternal silence of the Emperor, now watching over us in
spirit instead of in person, we will endure. There will be no
more war on such a perilous scale. There will be an end
to wanton destruction. Yes, foes will come and
enemies will arise. Our security will be
threatened, but we will be ready, our
mighty fists raised. There will be no
great war to challenge us now.
We will not be brought
to the brink like that
again...

PROLOGUE

The void

The Imperium's eyes did not sleep. They did not blink. Even as the body convulsed with agony, wounded to the core by the Beast, the eyes watched. Organic or augmetic, sentient or servitor, the eyes watched the human galaxy without rest. They were everywhere.

Almost everywhere.

They were not here.

Here was night in its purest form. The black of the void was profound, an abyss of infinite depth, the sparks of the stars merely cold, jagged stabs. There was no true light here. There was only its dust, its ashes, the glint of the past that was years and centuries and thousands of millennia old.

No light. No warmth.

No watchers.

But if there had been, they would have seen the ork fleet surround the dark world. The orks did not make planetfall. They bombarded the surface with missiles and shells. They scorched it with energy beams. The ground ran with molten tears. Glows of orange and crimson, false sunrise and false sunset, spread their rage across the land. The planet shook. It cried out in its pain.

The orks' target weathered the bombardment. It did not cry out. It was implacable in its silence.

And the orks did not land.

They battered the world with even greater ferocity. They brought light to the planet, and it did nothing but burn and shatter.

But they did not land.

The hurled their hatred at their target. They sought to make it scream and die. It remained silent.

Yet it answered the orks. It answered with fury.

ONE

Terra – the Imperial Palace

The silence crept through the halls and into Koorland's mind. There was no lack of noise in the chamber, but the silence found the cracks between the hiss of steam, the crackle of energy, the clanking of mechadendrites. The silence was strong. It was filled with the dead, and with futility. Koorland wondered if this same silence had blanketed Terra in the wake of the Proletarian Crusade. It was a quiet deeper than mourning, more powerful than despair. It had followed him from Ullanor. It had been waiting for him on Terra.

Its weight was crushing.

The chamber was part of a bulbous chapel on the west side of the Cathedral of the Saviour Emperor's exterior wall. The space was an ecumenical one, an architectural statement of the essential identity of the Imperial Creed and the Cult of the Omnissiah. The Black Templars of the Last Wall had insisted the decryption of the visual feed occur on sacred ground. Its transmission had been among the last

acts of a Venerable Brother, and it had emerged from a battle where many Black Templars had died.

The chapel did double duty as site of worship and laboratorium. It would serve. The Mechanicus adepts fed the data through cogitators, assisted by Black Templars serfs. The air was thick with incense.

The operation was performed under the supervision of Eternity. He was of the Last Wall now, and wore the colours of the Imperial Fists, but he had come from the Black Templars. His arms were folded, his head bowed in reverence.

Koorland watched from the rear of the chapel with Thane. They were alone. Eternity had refused to allow any of the High Lords to bear witness, and Koorland did not blame him. Their presence would have disturbed the solemnity of the ceremony. Though Koorland did not care for the religiosity of the ritual, he accepted it. Even if he hadn't, he would have barred the High Lords. There was no place for them and dignity to coexist.

'Any speculations?' Koorland asked Thane.

'None.' The Chapter Master of the Fists Exemplar spoke with a grim, flat tone. He sounded like a man bracing himself for the worst.

'We know it is important. And to our advantage, if it emerged from a victory against the orks.'

'I know,' said Thane, as if Koorland had pointed out what he most dreaded.

Koorland said nothing else. Thane was surrounded by his own version of the crushing silence. Koorland could not dispel his own. There was nothing he could do for the Exemplar.

The silence settled over them. The chanting of the tech-priests and the crackle of energy discharges did little to pierce it. Koorland watched the ritual, but barely saw it. His vision narrowed to a dark tunnel. His consciousness sank into the tunnel and he stayed there, numb. The suffocation of the silence held off the piercing blade of loss, guilt and defeat for the moment. It was not a respite. It was only a different quality of pain.

He was so far in the tunnel he didn't realise at first that he was being addressed.

'Lord Commander Koorland,' the voice repeated, its augmetic larynx buzzing.

Koorland blinked. The chapel snapped back into place about him. He looked down at the adept. Her name was Segorine. A cluster of servo-arms, segmented so that they flexed like tentacles, emerged from her torso. Her face was a steel mask dominated by compound eyes.

'The decryption is complete,' Segorine said.

'Thank you,' said Koorland. He and Thane followed her down the chapel aisle to where the other tech-priests waited. Behind the altar, a large pict screen pulsed with snow.

'Faith,' said Eternity.

Koorland waited.

'Faith,' Eternity said again. 'That is what we are about to witness. That is what will grant us victory against the Beast.'

'I see,' Koorland said, noncommittal.

Segorine snaked out a limb to a control panel built into the altar. She depressed a dial, and the screen came to life. The images flickered and jumped, and the muzzles of beam weapons flared everything to white. Explosions broke up the picture.

But the worst distortion came from unleashed psychic energy. Koorland saw the Black Templars at bay, fighting hard against the ork horde. He saw the greenskin psyker, its power ferocious, seeming to destroy reality along with the images. He saw the Black Templars pray as they fought. The sound was a riot of distortion, a grating rhythm barely recognisable as gunfire. Breaking through in fragments were deep, sonorous chants, magnified by vox-casters. The voices of faith travelled across destruction and time to frame their moment of victory.

For a moment, the sound cleared altogether. The yowls of the orks and the concussions of the guns vanished. There was only the stern, martial prayer of the Black Templars. The energy flares of the witch stuttered, then spread out as if they had hit a wall. They curled away from the Space Marines. Koorland leaned forward, astonished. Arcing waves of power slammed back into the greenskin psyker. The beast's mouth opened wide, its face contorted, and still there was only the sound of the chanting. The ork's eyes burst. It exploded into flame. The energy flashed across the frame of the feed, utterly uncontrolled, blasting every ork to ash. The energy storm swallowed up the chanting. The chapel filled with a shattering feedback shriek, and the visual feed disintegrated.

The screen returned to snow, then went black.

'The visible energy,' Thane said slowly. 'I didn't see it come from the Black Templars.'

'No,' Koorland agreed. 'It was all from the ork psyker.'

To the tech-priests he said, 'Will you play that back again? Slowly.'

They watched. At the end, Thane said, 'Are the orks and their witches linked?'

'In some way, they must be,' said Koorland. He could see no other interpretation. The psyker's death had triggered the immolation of the horde.

'So if we can target their psykers...'

'A possible weakness, yes.' Koorland turned to Eternity. 'That was not the work of a single warrior, was it?' Certainly not a Librarian. The Black Templars allowed no psykers within the ranks of their battle-brethren.

'That was the faith of all my brothers present in that battle,' said Eternity. 'A collective strength.'

'Against a single ork witch,' said Thane.

'Its fall destroyed its entire force,' Eternity pointed out.

'Yes,' said Koorland. 'Yes, it did.'

If only we'd known. The words came to him unbidden, a canker on his soul. He tried to push them away. He tried to tell himself the Imperial tactics on Ullanor would not have been altered, but his grief would permit no such comfort.

If only they had known. They would have fought differently. They would have made a greater priority of finding and taking out the ork psykers. They would have targeted the source of greenskin strength and turned it into a weakness.

He thought of Vulkan. The primarch had wished for the aid of the Sisters of Silence. He had recognised the need for a strong counter to the psykers.

He must have known, Koorland thought. He tried again to tell himself that they would not have fought any differently.

He knew that wasn't true.

Neither were many things, he thought, that he had been telling himself of late. He had worked hard to maintain an illusion of self that made it possible for him to carry the responsibility he had shouldered. It made it possible for him to lead. But he had led nowhere except to disaster. He had nothing but contempt for the High Lords. At this moment, though, he was not sure how he was any different from them.

He forced himself to focus on the moment. 'We may not see the key to the weakness in this data,' he said. 'But it *is* a weakness, and we *will* exploit it.'

But an hour later, he was still thinking about difference, his mind chasing itself in a toxic spiral. He walked alone on the ramparts of Daylight Wall, looking up into the night of Terra. There was a strong wind, and the sulphurous clouds over the Imperial Palace roiled, broke and reformed. In the gaps of their anger, the light of two moons reached down. Luna was a narrow, waning crescent. The reflected glow of the ork attack moon was paler, colder and more baleful. That threat was over, or at least contained. The orks were gone, the moon blockaded. But it was still a presence in the Terran sky, an insult and a wound to the heart of the Imperium. No enemy, even defeated, should ever have come so close.

He pictured another moon. He pictured several. Next time, the orks might not hold back from deploying their gravity weapons against Terra. They might have lost interest in conquest. They had been bloodied on Ullanor. Their vengeance might well take the form of total destruction.

And even if the moon was dead, it was not silent. It roared. *I AM SLAUGHTER. I AM SLAUGHTER. I AM SLAUGHTER.* The broadcast was ceaseless. It was gigantic. It would take nothing for Koorland to open a vox-channel and hear it.

He chose not to, but the reality of the shout was another poison in the toxic silence. The words of the Beast hammered at Terra, breaking down the spirit of its citizens. The roar mocked the sacrifices on Ullanor. It declared the futility of every Imperial endeavour to stop the orks. Every great quest, every journey, every challenge, every hard-won battle and shard of hope – they all meant nothing. What did they have to show for Caldera, for Ullanor? Even their victory against the moon was turned into mockery.

Koorland grieved, and so did all the world. He did not know fear, but he knew its cancer possessed every mortal soul on Terra.

The battlements of Daylight Wall were built upon many terraces. Turrets and cannon emplacements on multiple levels faced the east, so many it seemed they should be able to kill the rising sun if it dared to challenge the Emperor. Koorland walked along the top. He took up a position between the crenellations and looked down at the bristling strength below him. Not long ago, this perspective would have renewed his sense of duty and of purpose. Now he observed the defences and thought: Not enough.

The guns were insufficient.

So was he.

The approaching footsteps were quiet, more from a desire not to disturb than not to be heard. Koorland turned to the right. Drakan Vangorich, Grand Master of the Officio

Assassinorum, walked down the wide avenue of the wall towards him. There was enough room between the battlements for a Baneblade to pass, and the Assassin was a tiny figure in the night. On either side, the relief sculptures of the crenellations celebrated Imperial might. Heroic figures cut down their foes with sword and gun. Koorland's eyes went back and forth from the brutal strength of the stone to the wiry Grand Master. In the contrast, he felt a glimmer of inspiration. It passed before he could discern its shape.

Vangorich nodded to Koorland as he drew near. 'A homecoming?' he asked.

'No,' said Koorland. 'Daylight Wall Company is gone. And my duty is no longer named by a single battlement.'

'It was never limited to that, though.'

'No, it wasn't.' Koorland sighed. 'But there was great order in that naming. Symbols have powerful meaning.'

'As does their loss,' Vangorich said quietly.

'Yes.' The annihilation of Daylight Wall Company was of little importance next to the loss of a Chapter. And what was even that compared to the death of a primarch?

'I've seen the recording,' Vangorich said.

'For all the good it does us now.'

Vangorich gave him a sharp look. 'Defeatism doesn't suit you, Lord Commander Koorland.'

'Neither does naïveté,' Koorland said.

Vangorich was quiet for a moment. Then he said, 'It isn't that long since we last spoke on this wall.'

'It isn't, and I don't come here seeking to have my morale boosted by you.'

'It would be an odd thing to do, given my particular duty.'

Koorland grunted.

'I hope, though,' Vangorich went on, 'that you will listen to counsel.'

'I know what you would have to say about being a symbol.'

'And you would deny its truth.'

'I would deny my fitness to serve as that symbol.'

'Would you deny your duty to do so?'

'You know I would not,' Koorland growled. Duty and fitness were very different things, and he resented Vangorich's blurring of the two.

'No,' the Grand Master said. 'You have never turned from your duty. You have always done it. You did it on Ullanor too.'

'To no end.'

'And who would have been better suited? Who should have led instead?'

Koorland didn't answer.

'Vulkan left much of the campaign in your hands, didn't he?' Vangorich said.

'He did.'

'Was he wrong? Did he err?'

Koorland looked down at the Grand Master and glared. Again he said nothing. He could not bring himself to say aloud that Vulkan had been mistaken. He would not question the final decisions of the last primarch.

'I'll take your silence as a *no*,' Vangorich said.

'You're playing a game with words,' said Koorland. 'It isn't amusing and it isn't useful.'

'You're right,' Vangorich said, his tone suddenly sharp. 'There would be nothing useful in a game. The High Lords have proven this many times over, and as far as I can tell, they're very much intent on proving it yet again. I am not playing at anything. What we need right now is clarity, don't you agree?'

'I do.' He grimaced. 'We could have used the clarity of Magneric's information on Ullanor.'

'Exactly. Obfuscation, illusion, denial, ignorance, they have brought us disaster.'

So has everything else, Koorland thought. He said, 'Your point, when you reach it, will have to be an impressive one, Drakan.'

'Did Vulkan speak to you before the end?'

'He did.'

'And?'

Koorland took a deep breath. He let it out with a shudder, as if it could expel the burdens and memories that had built up like a toxic cloud inside his chest. 'He ordered me to carry on.'

'That was all?'

'He called me Lord Commander. He said I was the Imperial Fists.'

'And you would dismiss those words?'

Koorland shook his head. 'It isn't that simple.'

'I see nothing simple in what I am suggesting. I see that you have a great burden to carry, one that is enormously complex. It is yours, however. You shouldered it after Ardamantua. You have carried it since. Vulkan reaffirmed your duty to carry on. It is your burden, because you have the strength for it. The primarch saw you are the leader we need now. So do all your brothers. Across the Chapters.'

Koorland narrowed his gaze in disbelief.

'Your doubt has no place here, Lord Commander,' Vangorich said. 'Unless your information is more complete than mine. Has there been a challenge to your leadership? Has one of the surviving Space Wolves stepped forward to declare himself the alpha of the campaign?'

'No,' said Koorland. 'And I would thank you to refer to those Space Marines with greater respect. They have sacrificed much.'

'All have,' Vangorich said softly. 'And the mission was a disaster. Yet there has been no challenge. There is a reason for that. They see what Vulkan saw. They await your orders.'

'My orders.'

'I assume you aren't going to wait for the orks to attack first.'

Koorland felt the corners of his lips pull back. After a moment he realised something like a smile, cold and hard and hungry, had appeared on his face.

'You're very good at what you do,' he told Vangorich.

'I have to be.'

Koorland studied the Grand Master. 'Perhaps we should learn from you,' he said. As he spoke, the feeling of inspiration returned. It was stronger now. Closer to being something he could articulate.

'What do you think I could teach you?'

'Precision,' Koorland said. The idea had almost formed. 'You rely on few to do work that affects many.'

'Precision is the correct word,' said Vangorich. 'What is necessary is not overwhelming force. What is needed is the right weapon and the right target.'

'Which we have lacked,' Koorland muttered.

'The weapon or the target?'

'Both. We thought we had found the Beast on Ullanor. Vulkan gave his life to slay it. And now...' He pointed at the attack moon.

I AM SLAUGHTER, said the silence.

Koorland felt the words without hearing them. He saw Vangorich wince, and knew the Grand Master felt them too.

'The Beast survived?' Vangorich asked.

'No. It can't have. Yet something with its voice lives on. And that palace on Ullanor...'

'Yes,' said Vangorich. He understood. The horror was not lost on him.

'They are creating an empire,' Koorland said. 'They plan to build it on the ashes of our own.'

Vangorich nodded. 'The ambassadors,' he said.

'What about them?'

'More evidence of the construction of an empire. The greenskins are evolving the classes that will be needed for an empire to function.' He nodded to himself again. 'So,' he said, 'no matter what died on Ullanor, the force of the Beast lives on. We have to consider what this means for our strategy.'

'Our attack was too blunt. We were not a surprise. The orks knew what was coming, and prepared for us.'

'What do you conclude, then?'

'We need to keep looking for the Beast. In whatever form the guiding power of the orks exists, let us call it that. If we destroy it...'

'The ork empire will fall,' Vangorich finished. 'A

decapitation. You need to commit yourself to that, Lord Commander.'

'We are. We were. We have to change our methods, though. If we come at the orks again as we did, even if we could assemble such a force again, they will win again. They out-number us, and they outgun us.' The last admission was the hardest. The entire history of the Imperium's fight against the orks had involved the superiority of humanity's tech-nology against the orks' vast tide of savagery. Recognising that the orks' technology had outstripped the Imperium's was a perpetually reopened wound. It had been the most basic fact of the war since Ardamantua, but speaking the words aloud sounded perilously close to capitulation. Not to face that reality would lead to true defeat. 'We have to hit them another way.'

The inspiration that had teased the edge of his conscious-ness burst upon him. It had the clarity of revelation. He had known the same certainty when he had called for a unified command of the Imperial Fists Successor Chapters. Then, as now, the epiphany had come in the wake of devastating loss. Then, as now, he saw his course of action allowed for no doubt. He might question his own worthiness. He knew he would. But the path to follow shone before him.

He did not look at what he must do as cause for hope. It might yet fail. It was, instead, the thing that must be done. It was the one move left that the orks might not be able to counter.

'Sometimes,' Vangorich said, unknowingly giving voice to Koorland's revelation, 'a single knife can be more effec-tive than a broadsword.'

'Yes,' Koorland said. '*Yes*. As your Officio has shown throughout its history. I'm interested in your tactics, Drakan. We need to learn from them. *That* is the counsel I would welcome from you.'

'The Adeptus Astartes are not assassins,' Vangorich said. He sounded cautious. 'There are paths we must be careful not to take, if we do not want to repeat mistakes a thousand years old.'

'We aren't assassins,' Koorland agreed. He respected Vangorich, but more, the Grand Master was the one member of the High Council for whom he felt anything even remotely approaching trust. He respected Veritus and Wienand, but he did not trust either. They were too immersed in the political machinations of the ordos. Veritus, in particular, he did not trust to act as the needs of the immediate crisis dictated. But now, as Vangorich spoke, Koorland saw the politician emerge in him. His caution was genuine. Even so, Koorland sensed an instinctive territorial defence.

Vangorich did not have to worry. Koorland had no interest in assassination. Decapitation was still the goal. And now he could imagine a new means to that end.

'I don't want to know about your organisation, your weapons or your specific tactics,' Koorland said. 'I want to hear about the broader strategy. Your philosophy of war.'

Vangorich gave him a half-smile. 'You think the Officio Assassinorum goes to war?'

'Of course it does, even if it might use a different name.'

Vangorich parted his hands, conceding the point. 'Go on,' he said.

'Tell me about the knife, and how it strikes.'

TWO

Terra – the Imperial Palace

Wienand sat in the lowest gallery of the Great Chamber. She had what amounted to a private stall. It had not been built as such; rather, a large fall of rubble had sectioned this small area of the benches from the other tiers. None of the minor lords who still attended council sessions had attempted to lay claim to it. Many likely did not even know about it. The heaps of tumbled marble and rockcrete shielded it from view of the other tiers. It was easily visible only from below, on the floor of the Chamber. If any of the nobility or Administratum officials were aware of this corner, they ignored it, preferring not to sit alone, and so Wienand had it for herself. She was unseen by the other spectators, and she had a good view of the dais.

Around the Chamber, the banners of the Imperium hung at half mast. So did every banner on every spire of the Imperial Palace. Green bands adorned the arms of the High Lords and of the spectators. The Council, the Palace and all of Terra mourned the loss of the last primarch.

Wienand knew that for many, it was not a pure form of grief. It was coloured by too much fear.

Veritus sat with the Council. Wienand was the joint Inquisitorial Representative, but she was content to be away from the dais today. The truce with Veritus was holding. They had not signed a peace accord, but they had found a way of working together. She could make her voice heard again, and, more importantly, she could watch the Council work through its contortions. Being at one remove from some of the debates was useful. It granted her perspective. She could observe the currents of the struggles, the developing fault lines, the weaknesses and pressure points.

All information was useful, she thought. All knowledge was power. In the present crisis, there were limits to what anyone, in the Council or outside it, could accomplish. She was determined to push against those limits. She would do what was needed to safeguard the Imperium.

Koorland, she could see, held fast to the same philosophy. The last Imperial Fist's armour was polished, but bore the marks of the battle on Ullanor. The ceramite was cracked from bullet impacts, scarred by blades, scorched by flame. Koorland's face bore the traces of almost as many wounds. His genhanced physiology had healed them, the new flesh roughened and thick. Koorland towered over the High Lords, but it was more than his height that made him the dominant force on the dais. It was more, too, than the fact he had fought and bled for the Imperium. He was not the only veteran on the dais. Abel Verreault, the Lord Commander Militant of the Imperial Guard, Lord High Admiral Lansung, Vernor Zeck, the Grand Provost Marshal of the

Adeptus Arbites – all had their own scars of war. Zeck had lost much of his original flesh.

Perhaps it was the degree of Koorland's sacrifice. Perhaps it was the scale of his loss, immeasurably beyond the trivialities of corporeal injury. He had lost his Chapter. And now, after the almost inconceivable casualties on Ullanor, after the death of the last primarch, what he had not lost was his inflexibility of purpose and his aura of command. What he announced to the High Lords had the weight of law.

They're going to fight you on this one, she thought. They're going to fight very hard indeed.

'I don't understand,' said Tobris Ekharth, Master of the Administratum. 'You're talking about a united mission of the Adeptus Astartes? How is that different from what was already attempted on Ullanor?'

Wienand stifled a cynical chuckle. Koorland had barely begun to lay out his vision, and Ekharth was interrupting. Perhaps he was already confused. She didn't think so. He was already anticipating where Koorland was going, and was impotently trying to stop him from speaking those words.

The Space Marine looked at Ekharth, his face stony with contempt.

'I have proposed no such thing,' Koorland said. 'I am calling for the creation of a new force entirely. We cannot use a blunt weapon against the orks. We must strike with precision, swiftly, giving them no chance to mount a defence. Our force will be composed of independent kill-teams. The members of each kill-team will be determined by the needs of the mission and will be drawn from across the Chapters.'

'Independent to what degree?' Zeck asked, sceptical.

'Completely autonomous with regards to the completion of the mission. Answerable to a centralised command.'

'And whose command would that be?'

'Mine.'

'Not the Council's?'

Wienand was impressed Koorland did not snort in disbelief. 'No,' he said.

'That's what I thought,' said Zeck.

'This is monstrous,' said Mesring. The Ecclesiarch of the Adeptus Ministorum spoke with a trembling voice. The tremor was so pronounced, he barely managed a croak. His skin had a bad sheen to it. When he leaned close to the other Lords, their faces twitched as if they were holding their breath.

Before Mesring could speak again, Juskina Tull jumped in. 'Exactly,' she said. 'It *is* monstrous.'

The authority of the Speaker for the Chartist Captains had been in ruins since the disaster of the Proletarian Crusade. Wienand wondered if she saw an equivalence in Ullanor, and a chance to regain ground at Koorland's expense.

'Monstrous,' Koorland repeated.

'You are using this crisis for the political gain of the Adeptus Astartes,' Tull said. 'We have not forgotten why the Legions were broken up into the smaller Chapters. And now you would bring together *all* the Adeptus Astartes under a single authority, answerable only to you?'

Koorland's eyes narrowed. 'You are wilfully misunderstanding me,' he said. He spoke calmly, but Wienand could hear the rumble of anger in his deep voice. 'The force will consist exclusively of mission-specific kill-teams. These are not armies. They will not be engaging the orks in great fields of battle. That is the strategy that has failed us. We must think otherwise, and wage a new kind of war, or face annihilation.'

'Of course you are not proposing unification,' Lansung said. 'You know the Council would never accept it. Furthermore, the casualties on Ullanor were too great to permit a mass assembly. You are being disingenuous. We can see where this path leads. Once these teams are formed, there will be nothing provisional about them. Consolidation will follow.'

Vangorich snorted. 'You're taking a lot for granted,' he said. 'So the Blood Angels and the Ultramarines will happily consent to submit to the authority of the lone Imperial Fist?'

Lansung waved the objection away. 'If the plan is moving ahead, then the internal politics have been resolved.'

'This is a coup!' Ekharth shouted. 'It will not succeed! We will not allow it!'

'Monstrous.' Mesring had not moved on from his initial judgement. The Ecclesiarch stood up from his seat, quivering, shaking his head back and forth like a wounded animal. 'Monstrous, monstrous.'

'Why?' Vangorich asked.

Mesring snapped his mouth shut. Still quivering, he looked at Vangorich with wide, nearly maddened eyes. He stared at the Grand Master of the Officio Assassinorum for several long seconds. Then he said, 'It cannot work. It will never work. It is against the divine will. It must never be attempted. It is unholy. Unholy.' He paused. He looked up at the dome of the Chamber. 'Unholy,' he said again, more quietly, more to himself than to Vangorich.

Wienand leaned forward, watching Mesring carefully. There was something wrong with him. She couldn't tell if the shaking was due to mental paroxysm or physical debilitation. Perhaps both. There had been fear in the look he had given Vangorich, yet his need to speak his truth had won out. Only his truth sounded odd. The other High Lords articulated their fears, and Wienand thought they were wrong. How they imagined the Dark Angels and the Space Wolves surrendering their independence was beyond her, but she could understand the logic of their anxieties. From her vantage point, just far enough away to see the entire Council at a glance, she could picture the High Lords as game pieces on a regicide board, the moves of one blocking and shaping the moves of the others, the ones with the least current power feeling they were the most vulnerable, and so making the most aggressive attacks.

Mesring, though, was puzzling. She should have been able to place him easily. He should, in this context, have been one of the more quiet members of the Council. The Ecclesiarchy had little to say when it came to strategy. As long as the orks were defeated, its power was unlikely to be diminished. Its only true fear should be the triumph of the greenskins.

So why was he frightened? she wondered. What possible threat would the kill-teams be to him?

Why? she wondered.

No, she corrected herself. She was asking the wrong question. It was assuming Mesring was acting out of the same self-preserving, territorial motives as the other High Lords. The assumption was wrong. Mesring's dismay at Koorland's plan was genuine. Wienand saw true religious horror in his reaction. He believed in what he was saying.

How could this possibly be against the Emperor's will? That was the question to ask.

It had no answer.

The other High Lords were wrong-footed by Mesring's reaction too. They did not appear to know how to respond. Even Tull was thrown off. She had tried to build on his horror from a political perspective. She clearly did not know how to do so from the perspective of faith. Wienand wasn't sure of the depth of Tull's piety, but it didn't matter. Whatever theological turn Mesring had taken, no one else present could follow him.

Abdulias Anwar ignored the Ecclesiarch completely. The Master of the Adeptus Astra Telepathica spoke as calmly as Koorland. His voice was a barely audible sibilance, insinuating rather than commanding. It wrapped itself around Wienand's will and tried to make itself one with her consciousness. She was used to being on her guard in the presence of Anwar, and she raised mental barriers, consciously pushing away the words of the telepath. She saw the slight shifting of positions on the dais as the other High Lords assumed their own forms of wary readiness.

'I cannot speak to matters of faith,' Anwar said. 'I will speak to matters of principle. What the Lord Commander of the Imperium proposes is the destabilisation of the governance of the Imperium.'

Relief washed over the Council. Anwar had returned

sanity to the debate. The ground was familiar once again. The opposition was clear. One after another, the High Lords railed against Koorland. They were unified in their accusations. Wienand found the unity significant. They were frightened. They saw his plan as a power play, not a strategy. They attributed their own motives to him.

The war, she saw, had taught them nothing.

Not all the High Lords spoke. Kubik and Veritus were quiet. The Fabricator General's servo-motors clicked. His optics whirred as they turned from one member of the Council to another. Most of the time, his attention was on Koorland. Veritus was just as intent on the Space Marine. They were listening and evaluating. They did not support his position, but they did not take a stand against it. They were seeing possibilities, Wienand thought. So was she. The potential for Koorland's force beyond the immediate need was amorphous.

'Cross-Chapter kill-teams will have no reason to exist beyond the present crisis,' Koorland was saying now. 'There will be no need for them, and the circumstance that makes their formation possible will cease to hold sway.'

'You cannot believe that,' Zeck said. 'If you go ahead with this madness, you will create a precedent. A pretext will always be found to keep the teams in place. That's why this can't happen even once.'

Correct, Wienand thought. On this point, the High Lords were right to be worried. If the kill-teams were successful, there was no way such a weapon would be put away.

If they were successful, she thought. Then what?

The great potential refused to come into focus. The force

had to be a reality first. She had to witness what it could do. Then she would know what else it might accomplish, and perhaps how it might be controlled.

'Vote, then,' Koorland snapped. 'Vote and be damned.'

The High Lords voted. Vangorich supported the plan. Kubik and Veritus abstained. The others voted against it.

Koorland did not hide his disgust. 'You're fools,' he said.

'We would be to fall into your trap,' Ekharth said, smug in victory.

Wienand waited for Koorland to punch the little man's head from his shoulders. The act would have confirmed the High Lords' worst suspicions, but it would have been warranted. Instead, Koorland strode from the dais.

'What do you plan to do?' Zeck called.

Koorland stopped. He faced the Council. His stillness became dangerous. Wienand was acutely conscious of what he could do to the High Lords if he were not holding himself back.

'I will do what must be done,' Koorland said. And as he turned once more to go, he added, 'So will you.'

'I understand your frustration,' Alexis Mandrell said, speaking into the vox-unit on his desk. 'I share it. But unless and until Admiral Lansung issues new orders, here we are.' The captain of the cruiser *Sybota*, commanding the blockade of the attack moon, was in his private quarters. He leaned back in his chair and put his feet up on his desk. Another twenty-four-hour cycle had been completed, and it had been another cycle of routine exercises. The endless broadcast of *I AM SLAUGHTER* from the moon was unchanging.

Mandrell had ordered the transmission blocked from all ships for the sake of morale, instituting an hourly verification that there had been no change in the message.

There was none.

'The task is dull,' he said. 'It's still necessary.'

'I'm not questioning that,' replied Captain Makayla Ochoa, of the frigate *Cyzicus*. 'It's the decisions that have *made* this necessary I don't understand. Such a large concentration of forces in this vicinity when reinforcements are desperately needed elsewhere...'

'You aren't the first to notice this, captain.'

'You don't say.' Ochoa had two decades more experience in the field than Mandrell, but her family was a far more minor noble house than his. They had served together in the Navy long enough that they acknowledged the political realities of the differences in their advancement with amused cynicism. Ochoa took the liberty of being as insubordinate as she pleased with Mandrell in private. He accepted this liberty as her due.

'I do say,' he answered.

'You have family connections to Lansung...' Ochoa began.

'Stop!' Mandrell held up a hand as if Ochoa could see him. 'No. No. There's no point, and I'm not using what capital I might *hypothetically* have to push for something that will go nowhere at best and result in embarrassment at worst.'

'Yours?'

'That I could survive. I mean the Lord High Admiral's. Do you think it's by his choice that we don't destroy that xenos hulk? The Mechanicus wants it. If the Lord High Admiral has not ordered us to destroy it, it's because he can't. I'm not going to put him in the position of having to admit that. I like my command. If it were possible to send us elsewhere, he would have done so.'

'Really.' Ochoa did not sound convinced.

'Really.' Mandrell did his best to be emphatic. In truth, he wasn't sure. The Imperial Navy's dispositions had been erring on the side of caution since the start of the war.

'So keeping a massive fleet presence in the vicinity of Terra, where it is unlikely to suffer any losses, has nothing to do with shoring up his position on the Council?'

'No. Captain, you will cease this line of questioning.' Their vox-communication was encrypted, but Mandrell did not trust it that much.

Ochoa snorted. 'My apologies,' she said. Dryly.

'We'll see all the combat we could hope for,' Mandrell said. He was telling the truth, though he suspected Ochoa would interpret his words differently than how he thought of them. He was not displeased to be assigned to a pointless blockade. The *Sybota* had been on no more than the edges of the engagements with the orks, and that had been enough. He did not think he was a coward. He simply did not see the value in plunging into battles where the only likely outcome was annihilation. Let the Adeptus Astartes take the lead in suicidal missions. That was their strength. Let the Imperial Navy consolidate gains and hold reclaimed systems. There was no dishonour in that service.

He couldn't dispute Ochoa's contention that resources were misallocated, but he had seen enough campaigns to know there was nothing new there. If poor deployment decisions were to continue, he would prefer them to work in his favour.

'So we're here indefinitely,' Ochoa said. 'How are we–'
She stopped. 'What was that?'

'What did you...' Mandrell began. Then he heard and felt
something that began as a deep, rattling vibration. It ran
through the deck and wall of the *Sybota*. The data-slates on
his desk drummed against the surface. The vibration ran up
through the frame of his chair and through his spine. It grew
stronger. A sweeping vertigo shook him, and he almost slid
to the ground. He switched the vox to the bridge channel.
'What is happening?' he bellowed.

He couldn't hear his own voice. The rattle had built to a
piercing metallic scream. The entire ship howled in agony.
Blood burst from Mandrell's nose and ears. The vertigo grew
worse. He clutched the desk, disoriented as his sense of up
and down spiralled. He forced himself upright and staggered towards the door of his quarters, weaving with every
step. As he reached the door, a colossal boom cut through
the *Sybota*'s shriek. The sound was so vast it sucked the
air from his lungs. He fell to his knees. The deck heaved.
He dragged himself forward, clutched at the doorway and
hauled himself up.

He stumbled into the corridor. The echoes of the boom
faded, swallowed by the grinding scream of metal and the
thunder of cracking stone. The walls, deck and ceiling of
the corridor buckled. Pulverised marble filled the air. Mandrell coughed, inhaling dust and smoke. The lumen orbs
flickered off and on. Ruptured conduits spewed steam and
flame. He made his way forward, unable to see more than
a few metres ahead. He saw the shapes of crew moving
through the haze, trying to run. They flailed as the deck rose

and fell like an ocean in a storm. The agony of the vessel was deafening. Mandrell could hear no voices or warning klaxons. The silhouettes of his crew were pantomimes of crisis.

The weight was sudden, terrible, crushing. It came upon Mandrell like the fall of a huge wave. It smashed him to the deck. His ribs cracked. His nose and teeth shattered. He was immovable, held fast to the deck by his own impossible mass. Struggling against the prison of gravity, he raised his head just enough to look ahead. He could do no more, but even this victory was enough. It meant he saw what happened next.

The scream of the *Sybota* was transcendent. The cracking was the sound of a world coming apart. Power failed. The lumen orbs flickered out. The corridor went dark, lit only by the flicker of spreading flame. Then, summoned by the cracking and the grinding, a new light burst into brief, monstrous life. Mandrell stared into a blinding flare of fire and energy discharges. And then there was the wind, blowing past him with a hurricane's roar. And then there was the cold.

Wind and cold, because the *Sybota* tore in half.

Mandrell stared in wonder and horror. He had that much time. His final breath was long enough for him to see the fore section of the cruiser fall away from the aft. He saw all the exposed decks of his vessel. He saw plasma explode along the edges of the wound. He saw thousands of crew and troops float off into the void, tiny figures, insignificant, a tumbling swarm. He saw the dark of the void snuff out the flames, but the light did not die at once. The void shields went first, their end a chain reaction of brilliant ferocity, the ship's defences exploding outward, failing after the hull itself.

The *Sybota* was a broken bone, its two halves slowly turning away from each other. The vision was immense. Mandrell witnessed a death so great, his own end was meaningless. The seconds that remained to him were consumed with bleak wonder.

Then the wind ceased, and there was only the dark, and the merciless, terminal cold.

Ochoa reached the command gallery above the bridge in time to see the *Sybota* break in two. The ork gravity weapon had lashed out from the attack moon, a single whip of unfurled, impossible force. It had seized the cruiser, and its grip was doom. The beam had sideswiped the *Cyzicus*. The blow had been nothing, the mere wake of the passing force. It had still been enough to disrupt the frigate's artificial gravity, hurling Ochoa back and forth against corridor walls as she ran for the bridge. Klaxons still wailed, and the screens next to the oculus were filled with the red script of damage reports.

'All batteries,' Ochoa said. She got no further before there was another bright flash in the upper left quadrant of the oculus. The entire superstructure of the destroyer *Iron Castellan* vanished in the killing light. The ship began a slow roll out of formation. What looked like a small mountain had materialised in the vessel's core, its rocky peaks projecting out of the stern and the upper portions of the hull. Ochoa stared for several seconds at the impossible vision. Just before the greater flash came, consuming the vessel entirely, she understood.

Teleportation, she thought. They teleported a chunk of the attack moon into the *Castellan*.

'Signal all ships,' Ochoa shouted to Gliese, the officer of the vox. 'Open fire on the moon with all batteries, all torpedoes. Destroy it.'

Gliese turned to look up at her. 'We have orders to–'

Damn Lansung and damn the Mechanicus. If those flesh-less cultists wanted the greenskin toys, they could put them back together again. 'You have new orders from me. The responsibility is mine. Now do as I say or I'll shoot you where you stand.'

Gliese saluted and opened a channel.

'All vessels, open fire,' Ochoa said. 'Full batteries, full torpedo launches. Destroy that moon.'

'By whose authority...'

That was Huf, squawking from the frigate *Steadfast Contrition*.

'By mine,' Ochoa told him. 'As most senior surviving captain. Open fire, Huf, or do you want the greenskins to crush your ship?'

Huf clicked off.

Moments later, Ochoa saw the streams of shells and torpedoes streak from the blockade towards the attack moon. Imperial ordnance cut through the dark of the void. No one else questioned the order. The other captains had probably already been issuing their commands. They knew what was at stake.

The barrage was immense. It was also too late. Before the first torpedo struck the surface of the moon, its terrible maw began to open once more. The shouting, raging corpse had come back to life. From its interior came a swarm of ork ships. Interceptors, fighters, bombers and torpedo ships raced for the blockade. Dozens were caught by the oncoming artillery. The near space of the attack moon became a fiery nimbus of superheated plasma and disintegrating metal. Hundreds more greenskin vessels shot through the curtain of destruction.

Ochoa stared at the oculus, at the oncoming storm of predators. Almost unconsciously, her hand moved to the tacticarium table at her side. She tapped the command vox-unit, tuning to the huge band of frequencies broadcasting the roar of the Beast.

She had no wish to hear it. Yet the need to face the full truth of the moment was too strong. She had never turned from battle. She had always sought the full measure of duty.

But there was more that directed her actions at that moment. The gaping maw of the ork base transformed the inanimate into a living skull. The face had a monstrous pull. Its power was absolute. Ochoa felt her insignificance before the presence of the active, murderous sublime.

Behold me, that gaping visage commanded. *You bow before a god of stillness. I am a god of speed and violence. I am present. I am ascendant.*

She turned the vox on to hear the actual voice, to blot out the words the sight of the moon tried to insinuate into her soul.

Ochoa vowed to herself she would fight the reality of the threat, and her spirit was the equal to its false divinity.

'*I AM SLAUGHTER!*' boomed through the command gallery. '*I AM SLAUGHTER!*' It seemed the moon itself was shouting in the bridge. '*I AM SLAUGHTER!*' And slaughter came from the moon, scything into the blockade fleet. Hundreds of ships descended on the frigates and destroyers. The Imperial cannons shifted from attack to defence. Every ship visible in the oculus flashed bright with straining void shields and the dissipating fireballs of destroyed ork craft. The attackers perished in droves. But more and more and more emerged from the maw, an endless curse from the god of violence.

'*I AM SLAUGHTER! I AM SLAUGHTER! I AM SLAUGHTER!*'

The word became truth, and the truth burned the fleet.

Koorland walked the edge of the dais in the Great Chamber. He would not take his seat. He would not even stand by it. He would not associate himself with the High Lords. He understood that the realities of his position made the division he wished to enact a false one; he was part of the political machine of Terra now, whether he chose to admit it or not.

It would be close to a lie to say he accepted these facts. It was enough to say he knew them to be true. Today, he had to distance himself as much as he could from the rest of the High Lords. He was too disgusted to count himself of their number. If he sat in that chair, he might even derive the wrong sort of satisfaction from the inevitable turn the debate would take. He detested that temptation. It soiled and corrupted. If Koorland gave into it, he would truly be able to count himself a High Lord.

The thought was revolting.

He saw the sharp features and steel-grey hair of Wien-and in her tier seat. Once again, she had decided to put some physical distance between herself and the other Lords. Vangorich and Veritus were in their seats. Koorland half-wondered how they tolerated their positions. Whatever else he might say of Veritus, the inquisitor was a faithful servant of the ordos and of the Imperium. Koorland had no doubt he always acted from a foundation of firm belief. Perhaps Veritus' convictions were his form of armour. His need to pull the levers of power as he saw fit kept him in the political game. And Vangorich was the hunter on the political fields. He was where he needed to be.

Koorland was not. At least, not yet. If the High Lords would cease their posturing and accept what they all knew they had to accept, he could get on with his real duty – directing the blade that would decapitate the orks.

But the posturing must happen. Its inevitability was as certain as Daylight Wall.

'How can they be back?' Ekharth was saying. 'How can the orks be back? The moon was dead!' He pointed a trembling finger at Koorland. 'You said it was dead!'

Of course I did, Koorland might have said. That's why I demanded a blockade be maintained. He said nothing. Arguing with the little man would be a form of defeat. It would be descending to the level where nonsense was seriously debated.

'Teleportation,' Kubik said, more to himself than to Ekharth. He nodded his head, in satisfied agreement with his own deduction. 'Confirmed by reports of the destruction of the *Iron Castellan*. The *Veridi giganticus* must have employed their teleportation technology to repopulate their attack base. The infiltration capabilities are impressive. So much more to learn.' He abandoned all pretence of speaking to the Council and began to dictate into a recording unit built into one of his arms. 'Effective range remains the question. Based on present knowledge, it appears to be effectively unlimited. Without any indication of the origins of teleported bodies, we are forced to the most extreme hypotheses in the interests of strategic extrapolations.' His flat, machinic tones managed somehow to sound regretful. He switched into the whistles and screeches of binary.

'Can your teams stop this?' Lansung asked Koorland. His fleet was bleeding and dying. Already, a third of the vessels surrounding the moon had been destroyed. Lansung sounded desperate.

'They will,' said Koorland.

'How do you know?' Ekharth shouted. 'This has never been done before! You have nothing to go on.'

Koorland stopped pacing. This time he would speak. He turned slowly to face Ekharth. 'They are Adeptus Astartes,' he said. 'I have that to go on. I need no more.'

'But...' Ekharth began. He trailed off and looked away from Koorland's glare.

Koorland faced Lansung. 'How long can the blockade hold?' he asked.

'Not long.'

'I noticed you have pulled the *Autocephalax Eternal* back to orbit around Terra. And that you are not sending reinforcements.'

'We can't. If the orks break through–'

'*When*, you mean,' Vangorich corrected.

'The defence of Terra is paramount,' Lansung said.

'Of course,' Koorland said. What the Lord High Admiral said was true. It was also convenient. Lansung's reluctance to commit the flagship *Autocephalax Eternal* to combat had moved far beyond the craven into a realm so contemptible it did not have a name.

'The kill-teams must act quickly,' Lansung said.

'They will,' Koorland said.

Mesring had been staring into the middle distance, distracted by inner visions Koorland couldn't guess at. Now the Ecclesiarch started in his seat. 'We have not voted!' he said. 'Nothing has changed! What was monstrous before is just as monstrous now.'

Silence from the other High Lords greeted Mesring's outburst. He looked from one to another, pleading for support that had evaporated.

Zeck sighed. 'What assurances do we have this will not be your coup?'

Vangorich laughed. 'And would you believe those assurances if you had them? Would they mean anything coming from any of you?'

Zeck said, 'You find our circumstances amusing?'

'Hardly,' said Vangorich, suddenly cold. 'Your responses to them, though, are quite another matter.'

'Only one response interests me,' Koorland. Even there he was stretching a point. He had little interest in anything the Council might say or do. He was here out of brute necessity and for no other reason. 'You know what you have to do. Vote or be damned.'

'You knew,' Ekharth said, sullen with revelation. 'You knew the orks would come back. You arranged this crisis. Now we have no choice but to embrace your rule as our salvation.'

'Shut up, Tobias,' said Tull. She sounded just as sullen, but where Ekharth was slipping into outright paranoia and speaking from genuine fear, in Tull's voice Koorland heard suspicion shaped by frustrated ambition. 'Let's get this over with.'

'No!' Mesring shouted. 'We must not let this pass! It is blasphemous!'

For the first time in the proceedings, Veritus spoke. 'How?' he asked.

Mesring hesitated. 'It is blasphemous,' he said again. He looked away from the inquisitor. He shrank against the back of his seat, staring at the floor.

Koorland frowned. Mesring's objections bothered him more than Ekharth's. The form they took made no sense. Koorland did not understand what was behind them, and that worried him.

The High Lords voted.

Mesring was the only one opposed. Even Ekharth, seeing himself isolated, joined with the others in voting with Vangorich. Veritus and Kubik abstained again. They seemed, Koorland thought, to have deliberately moved themselves to the sidelines. They were observers of an event whose end result could not be affected by their participation, and so they chose to guard their neutrality. They would bear watching. The power games of the High Lords never ceased, and it was the silent ones who were most formidable. They were the ones who, if they had not already seized an advantage, saw the potential of one within their grasp.

The Council feared Koorland's long-term plans. He wondered how the consequences of what he was about to set in motion would serve Kubik and Veritus. Like the Council, he had no choice.

Koorland left the dais without a word.

THREE

Terra – the Imperial Palace

Robed, Abathar gazed at the armour he was about to don once more, and thought of the task ahead. He was standing on the precipice of meaning. He needed to understand the nature of his leap, and his armour was the key to that understanding. He knew this at a deep level, one without words – one at the same depths as that which resonated with the needs of the machine-spirits when he listened to their rages and pains.

Outside the Techmarine's armorium, footsteps rang up and down the corridors of the Imperial Palace barracks reserved for the Dark Angels. He heard the careful tread of Chapter-serfs. He heard the mechanical trudge of servitors. He heard the metallic cacophony of repairs, the murmur of prayers, and the whisper of oaths. Shadows, flickering in torchlight, moved over the armour and its folded servo-arms. The restless dark was deep, rich with imminent knowledge.

The revelation was approaching.

The sounds of the mobilisation seemed hollow and sparse. So many empty armoria and meditation cells. So many brothers lost. It would be easy to hear, in the diminishment, the echo of defeat. After a loss, a smaller muster, a weakened force.

That would be a lie, he thought.

It was true the combined Chapters on Terra could not attack the orks as they had before. It was true the new strategy Koorland had proposed was the product of necessity.

'Not the full truths,' the Techmarine muttered.

'Lord?' one of his armament serfs asked. They were standing by, waiting for him to permit them to return to their work of repair. His armour had escaped critical damage on Ullanor, but it had been badly scorched by vehicle-mounted flamers. It was blackened across most of its surface. The livery of the Dark Angels awaited restoration.

'Wait,' Abathar said.

The full truth was that Koorland's plan would be a small deployment even if the disaster of Ullanor had never occurred. The plan had come into being through necessity, but its shape surpassed necessity. It was a new thing. In the demands it placed on the members of the kill-teams, it was an extraordinary thing. Abathar thought about the Space Marines at whose side he would be fighting. An Ultramarine. A Blood Angel. A *Space Wolf*. The composition of the teams was astounding. It would never have been possible before Ullanor.

Here again, was a product of necessity, and again the form of the act surpassed what was forced and entered into the realm of true daring and unprecedented innovation. Small squads of uniform composition would have been under-standable. There were enough survivors of each Chapter to have mounted operations on that scale. But Koorland was urging them all to go further. The orders were to forge squad-level bonds with Space Marines who were strangers to him and to the ways of his brothers. At least one, he would have regarded with so much suspicion he would have refused to be in the same room as that warrior in other circumstances.

The circumstances were beyond extraordinary. So was Koorland's plan.

'He is asking us to become something new,' Abathar said.

The squads were born of death, and their mission was death. They would be a lethal blade beaten to a point in the forge of tragedy.

Abathar watched the shadows on his armour, darkness shifting over black. The shadows appeared to him to be the shadows of his lost brothers. The fallen of Ullanor called to Abathar and to all the Adeptus Astartes making ready to wage war in a new way. *Look upon us,* they said. *Witness us, and strike in our name. See our death, and stand guard in our stead. See our death, and visit it upon our enemies.*

Born of shadow, Abathar thought, we become shadow. We are the eye of death.

He knew what he must do.

'Continue,' he said to the serfs. 'But the armour needs new colours.'

The man and woman looked at each other, then at Abathar, confusion spreading over their features.

'Restore the right pauldron,' Abathar said. It must remain

as it was, the icon of the Dark Angels pristine, the pride of brotherhood and Chapter still announced to the universe. 'Paint the rest black.'

'Lord?' the woman said again.

'You heard me.'

It had been over a thousand years since the Chapter had worn black livery. This darkness would be different, Abathar thought. It was the black of mourning. The black of anger.

The black of the death witnessed and delivered.

Koorland found the Fabricator General in the laboratorium of the Cathedral of the Saviour Emperor. Kubik was examining Magneric's data-feed again. When he saw Koorland approaching, he gestured to the three tech-priests attending him. They bowed and withdrew through doors at the far end of the chamber, angular limbs pistoning under their robes as they left.

Kubik turned off the feed as Koorland approached. 'What do you wish, Lord Commander?' he asked.

'I want to talk to you about the ork teleportation technology. I want us to use it against the attack moon.'

'That will not be possible,' said Kubik.

'Because it won't work?'

'The Adeptus Mechanicus is not the Departmento Munitorum, Lord Commander.' The voice was flat, mechanical, inhuman. And still it was contemptuous.

'Are we to rehearse our grievances once more?' Koorland asked. 'I had hoped we had put them in the past for the sake of the Imperium. You did not deny us the use of the gravity weapons on Caldera.'

'That technology was deployed by the adepts of the Mechanicus in that conflict. I heard no mention of their presence in your proposal.'

'Nor did I make one.'

'Then we have no more to say.'

'I'm surprised, Fabricator General. The teleportation of a body as large as the attack moon holds no interest for you, then?'

Kubik's stillness was the closest thing to uncertainty Koorland had ever detected in the High Lord.

'You are not planning to use the technology as an augmentation of our current teleportation capabilities?'

'No. Not primarily. We are going to teleport the moon out of this system.'

Kubik hesitated. It frustrated Koorland that he could not tell if the Fabricator General was evaluating the feasibility of the plan or formulating a lie.

'The possibility of success is minimal,' Kubik said at last. But he seemed less resistant now. He was being captured by the challenge of the problem.

'Why?'

'Our understanding of the technology is imperfect. Our adaptation is partial. The teleportation of Phobos was limited to repositioning it within its established orbit. The energy expenditure was of a magnitude very rare in a single action, requiring considerable resources on Mars. You wish to move a much larger body a much greater distance. We cannot transport the energy sources of Mars to the attack moon.' There was a squeal of binary. 'I amend my estimation. The operation is impossible.'

'We used the orks' energy sources against them on Caldera. We tapped into their grid to power the gravity weapon. We will do that again now.'

Kubik straightened in interest and surprise. 'Employ the attack moon's power to generate its own teleportation?'

'Precisely.' Koorland was aware of Kubik's optics examining him closely.

'The proposal is intriguing,' said Kubik. 'It has the merit of providing a testing ground for our advances.'

'It isn't a proposal,' Koorland said. 'It's an order.'

Kubik regarded him in silence, except for the low hum of servo-motors and calibrating sensors.

'This is what must be done,' said Koorland. 'We will neutralise the ork base once and for all. The Council has been too generous with regards to the desires of the Mechanicus. You had your chance to study it. Now here we are, with the orks on our doorstep once more, and the Navy falling before them. You have no more choice in obeying this order than I have in issuing it.'

Kubik's digits flexed and curled, flexed and curled. He said nothing.

He was still silent when Koorland left. But he had not refused again.

The initial muster for the kill-teams was held in the Monitus. Abathar had no difficulty in understanding the choice. The hall, with its statues of all the loyalist Legions, represented the ultimate unity of the Adeptus Astartes. He saw meaning in its position, so high above the Great Chamber. It was here, too, that Vulkan had shamed the High Lords.

It was a fitting place for the beginning of the new venture, and of a very particular kind of unity. One, he had heard tell, that the High Lords feared.

He arrived alone, following the orders of Grand Master Sachael.

'You are Dark Angels,' Sachael had told the survivors assigned to the kill-teams, 'but for the length of this mission, you will also be something else. You will fight with warriors you might have regarded as strangers, in any other situation. You cannot do so now. You will join them as brothers. So you must arrive at the Monitus alone. In this manner, you are not departing a squad or a company. You are joining something else.'

Abathar reached the top of the Stilicho Tower and entered the Monitus. He slowed as he approached his assigned position toward the centre of the balcony. He was not the first to arrive. A figure was standing at the rail, next to the Ultramarines statue, looking down at the roofs of the Imperial Palace. The right pauldron showed the icon of the Space Wolves.

But the armour was black. Abathar stopped three paces away. The Space Wolf heard him and turned around. Abathar faced the weathered, bearded features of Asger Warfist. The Wolf Lord blinked in surprise.

Neither Space Marine spoke. They acknowledged the importance of the moment with a solemn silence. Then Abathar said, 'This is not chance.'

Warfist nodded slowly. 'It is fate.'

When Abathar had entered the Monitus, there had been the low, echoing murmur of conversation. Now the sound was fading. Abathar saw Warfist's eyes shift, looking past him to the rest of the hall. They widened. Abathar turned.

There were more warriors in black armour. Abathar counted four others. Not many, but enough to be significant. Enough to prove the truth of Warfist's words. Fate was at work here. Its hand was visible to every warrior in the Monitus.

All conversation ceased. The only sound was the rap of boots against marble as the Space Marines in black moved to their positions. They were the focus of attention in the hall. Abathar felt the force of a dozen gazes fall on him. He was not troubled by the scrutiny, for he was as astonished as everyone else. He stared as hard as any of the others.

A seventh warrior in black arrived, this one a Blood Angel. Then an eighth, an Ultramarine.

Time in the Monitus paused. The hall filled with the power of significance.

Warfist stepped forward. He moved to the centre of the hall. He spoke, the wind-cured rasp of his voice stretching across the Monitus.

'Bear witness, brothers!' he called. 'Mark what is happening! This is a day the Imperium will remember.' He was one Space Marine among many, yet in declaring the importance of what was happening, he became its nexus. All eyes turned to Warfist. All voices spoke to him.

'An omen,' said another Space Wolf on the other side of the hall.

'It is more than that,' Warfist said.

'We have done this,' said Abathar. 'It is not visited upon us. We have taken this action. We have made this choice.'

'And the choice has weight beyond the acts of a single brother,' Warfist continued. 'One choice, multiplied. This is a truth.'

'So it is,' said a Blood Angel nearby. Abathar recognised him as Forcas. He had seen the name on the list of members of his designated kill-team. Forcas' armour was still red. 'Can any of us doubt this truth? When it appears to us so clearly, and with such force?'

'Was this truly a choice, then?' Abathar wondered. 'We were guided by the same circumstances, impulses and realities.'

'Perhaps we have made our own omen, then,' said Warfist. 'If we have, its weight is all the greater.'

Forcas was nodding. 'I will do as you have done,' he said.

'As will I,' the other Space Wolf shouted.

The call was taken up. The Monitus rang with the oaths of a grim unity. The individual squads came together. The assembled Space Marines formed an arc before Warfist and the great statues.

Abathar observed his fellow warriors with growing awe as the moments succeeded each other with ever greater import. There was never doubt as to the ultimate unity of purpose of all the Chapters of the Adeptus Astartes. Every battle-brother, no matter how estranged he might be from those in another Chapter, stood for the defence of the Emperor. On Ullanor, there had been the forging of many forces into one devoted to a single immediate goal. Here, though, was something else again. Here, the unity was not institutional. It was being forged at the level of the individual. There would be friction between members of the

kill-teams. Abathar had no illusions about himself, or how he would feel fighting in the same squad as a Space Wolf.

And yet...

What is this thing we are becoming?

Born of death. Forged in death. Living memoria of lost brothers, returning in anger.

'*What are we?*' Warfist roared. The question demanded an answer, but it was shouted with the certainty of the inevitability of that answer.

'We are witness!' said Forcas, and Abathar heard his thoughts present and past being spoken by others.

Here, now, we are one, he thought. We are this new weapon.

'We watch from death,' said the Ultramarine in black.

We are vigilance.

We are vengeance.

We are the judgement come for the xenos challenger.

There was such clamour in his mind, in his soul and in the hall that Abathar could not tell if the words came from within or without. Perhaps they were both. Internal need had led to an external manifestation on his armour, and on that of other battle-brothers. They were the example. They were the clarity of black.

Space Wolf, Dark Angel, Blood Angel and Ultramarine had spoken with a single voice.

'We are the Deathwatch!'

The words rang out above the others, given strength by their iron truth. It was a moment before Abathar realised the voice was his.

'Deathwatch!' Warfist repeated.

'Deathwatch!' said Forcas.

Deathwatch. The word, the name, the truth was shouted by every warrior in the Monitus. It was the moment of creation. That which had been shattered on Ullanor had taken on a new shape, renewed of purpose.

Deathwatch. It was a blade aimed at the throat of the Beast.

The clouds parted. The attack moon appeared, as if in anger at the challenge. The roars grew louder yet.

Deathwatch.

Abathar shouted the name, and it was a mission. It was a calling. It was an identity. Sachael had been correct. Abathar was a Dark Angel. Nothing would change that. Nothing could. But he was also this new thing. As his armour bore the colours of two allegiances, so did his being. There was no contradiction. The Deathwatch was formed of disparate pieces, and it would depend on their separate identities to create its own.

What have we become? The full answer would come in time. But the name was here, defined by the crucible of sacrifice and vengeance. The one and the many had become synonymous.

Deathwatch.

The refrain was a thunder strong far beyond sound. It shook the Stilicho Tower. It cracked the air over the Imperial Palace. It rose to the sky. Towards the attack moon. It was an answer to the endless shout.

I AM SLAUGHTER, the Beast exulted.

And the warriors of many Chapters said, *Fear us.*

* * *

'You want me to go back,' Galatea Haas said.

'Yes,' Koorland said.

They were in the barracks of the Adeptus Arbites. Despite her rise in rank, Haas spent most of her time in this quadrant. Her authority now extended to most of the Arbitrators still in the continent-sized palace. She was Proctor of the Primus Imperialis Division, and she looked exhausted. The numbers of the Adeptus Arbites had been so badly cut by the Proletarian Crusade that their efficiency was a shadow of what it had been. Haas' office reflected the constraints under which she laboured. It was bare except for a battered desk, a wooden chair, an equipment footlocker, and a massive vox-array.

Koorland found himself comparing the officer before him to the Grand Provost Marshal in the Great Chamber. He did not doubt Zeck's skill. His ability to process vast amounts of data was more than impressive, and he had a keen strategic mind. It was the uses to which Zeck's skill was put that inspired Koorland's contempt. Had Zeck ever been something more than the political animal he was now? Koorland had his doubts. To become a High Lord, Zeck would have had to concentrate first and foremost on the goals of his ambition. His effectiveness as an administrator would have been a by-product of his personal desires. In Haas, Koorland saw a career take the form of a calling. He recognised her driven gaze. It was a product of duty and of loss.

She greeted the news that she was being asked to return to the attack moon with a grim, tight-lipped calm, as if she had been expecting this conversation. She did not ask if she had a choice. She said, 'You're going inside again.'

'Yes, deeper. Small teams. This will be an infiltration.'

'I see. What is my role?'

'We will be looking for control centres and power sources. You are more familiar with the interior than anyone else still living.'

'I understand.' She tapped her shock maul where it hung from her belt. She took a breath. 'I shall be ready to embark when you command.'

'Thank you, proctor. It would have been understandable if you had been reluctant.' Understandable, though reluctance would not have kept her on Terra. She was needed, and Koorland had been prepared to order her participation in the mission. Presenting her with a request first had been a courtesy, and a mark of his respect for what she had survived and what she had accomplished. He was pleased the request had been enough.

'Reluctant?' Haas said. 'May I speak freely, Lord Commander?'

'Please do.'

'The prospect of returning there fills me with horror.' She spoke calmly, her voice and her gaze steady. There was a faint twitch in her right eye. It was the only expression of what she was really feeling. 'But I joined the Proletarian Crusade for a reason. I had a task, and that task is incomplete.'

'Your commitment to duty is admirable.'

Her mouth twisted. 'I'm not a saint,' she said. 'I lost my friends. I saw...' She faltered. The twitch became more pronounced. 'When the mountains moved...' She looked past Koorland, at something colossal. He knew what she was remembering – billions of civilians and troops crushed, turned into a towering wave of blood. He knew what had happened on the surface of the moon. He had not witnessed it, though he had seen other horrors on Ardamantua. He could empathise without being able to experience the precise nightmare. They had each gathered their individual scars.

'You want revenge,' Koorland said.

Her gaze sharpened again. She gave him a curt nod. 'I want to see the greenskins die in the same numbers. And I want to be responsible for that.'

'You will be,' Koorland promised.

The embarkation of the kill-teams took place in the Inner Palace's pocket space port. There were three squads heading for the attack moon. Each was to board a Thunderhawk bound for the Dark Angels strike cruiser *Herald of Night*, which waited at low anchor to take them through the warzone. The ship was the fastest of the Adeptus Astartes vessels present over Terra.

Vangorich watched the departure from the far western edge of the landing pad. The hot wind from the first of the Thunderhawks' turbofan engines blew his hair back. His eyes were painfully dry. Beside him, Wienand raised a hand to shield her eyes from the glare as a gunship turned on descent, its engines bright as suns in the pre-dawn gloom.

'They're all in black,' Wienand said, looking at the thirteen Space Marines.

'I've heard the change started with a few, and the others followed suit.'

'You have thoughts?'

'Koorland's force already has a distinct identity. Before the first battle.'

'A good sign, wouldn't you say?'

'For the task ahead, definitely.'

Wienand cocked her head. 'Interesting hedge. Wasn't this your idea in the first place?'

'It was,' he conceded.

The Thunderhawk's embarkation ramp lowered. Koorland crossed the landing, coming from an eastern entrance to the space port. He stopped in front of the gunship and faced the kill-teams. Thane was with him. Their armour was not black.

'Here's a difference,' Wienand said.

'Understandable,' said Vangorich. 'The continued existence of the Imperial Fists hangs by a thread. I can't imagine Koorland would do anything to downplay the memory of the Chapter.' The Imperial Fists livery was already the colour of mourning, he thought.

'Brothers,' Koorland said, his voice amplified by vox-casters around the periphery of the landing pad, 'you have earned my thanks many times over during the course of this war. You have fought, you have sacrificed, and you have followed me. What I see before me is something for which I cannot, in good conscience, express gratitude. To do so would be the height of arrogance. You have found the true meaning of our actions on this day. The Last Wall rose from ashes. So has the Deathwatch.'

'It has a name,' Vangorich said to Wienand. 'I've heard it more than once now. I didn't anticipate that when I spoke to Koorland. I didn't expect the identity to form so quickly or so definitively.'

'That's a problem?'

'The differences between a conception and its execution can be a source of unease.'

'I can't believe you're backing down from your position in the Council. You fought hard for this operation.'

'I know,' said Vangorich. 'And I still believe in it. This is our best hope now.'

'I'm still hearing *but* in your voice.'

'We are many, and we are one,' Koorland was saying. 'Today we will strike the greenskins in a manner they cannot anticipate, and in a manner that already surpasses anything I might have hoped for.'

The roar of the assembled Deathwatch forced Vangorich to wait before responding. When the noise subsided, Wienand spoke first. 'Surpassing hope isn't necessarily a good thing, is it?' she said.

He managed a tight, grim smile. 'Do you think it's entirely healthy for you to know me that well?'

'For you or for me?'

Either, he thought. He shrugged. 'The name. The colours,' he said. 'The black. I wasn't expecting any of that. So coherent an identity so soon...'

'The other High Lords anticipated this. Or something very similar.'

'True. That doesn't mean they were right about this force's long-term significance.' He became aware that Wienand was looking at him sharply.

'Altering livery isn't something the Adeptus Astartes do lightly,' she said.

'No. It may be a necessary gesture for this attempt to succeed.'

Wienand snorted. 'You don't believe that's all it is.'

'No, I don't.'

'We're witnessing the start of something that is going to be with us for a long time,' Wienand said. 'That's what is bothering you, isn't it?'

'It is,' said Vangorich.

'You don't really believe Koorland is planning a coup, though, do you?'

'I don't.' Vangorich sighed. 'It's not what he intends that's the problem. It's the thing he has created. The more successful the Deathwatch is, the more difficult it will be to disband. And Throne, we need it to be successful. But afterwards, what then?'

'You just implied you trusted Koorland.'

'If he doesn't survive,' said Vangorich. 'If his successor sees more potential for the Deathwatch than the immediate crisis...'

'Pessimist,' Wienand said.

'Pessimism is my duty,' said Vangorich. He looked at her. 'You don't seem worried.'

'I think you've been in the presence of the High Lords for too long, Drakan. They're a bad influence. Their thinking is constricting yours.'

'What do you mean?'

'I'm more intrigued by the possibilities than the dangers.'

'You think the Council's anxieties are groundless?'

'I didn't say that. If we consider them in the right light, they may in fact be the key to the possibilities.'

'Which are?'

'I'm not sure yet.'

Koorland had finished speaking and the first of the kill-teams had followed him into the Thunderhawk. It lifted off, and a second gunship descended to take on Thane and the next squad.

'I think we need to see how this day plays out first,' Wienand said. 'Don't you agree?'

'I do,' said Vangorich. She was right. And he did still believe in the effort under way. There were no other options left. Koorland had listened to his advice, and had adapted the philosophy of the Officio Assassinorum to the crisis, and to the Adeptus Astartes.

He had forged his blade.

'We are directing the primary data-feeds to your vox-frequency,' Adnachiel told Koorland.

'I am receiving them. Thank you, Company Master. I wish I could be on the bridge with you.'

'You are where you need to be,' Adnachiel said. Inside a Thunderhawk, inside a landing bay, he thought. He respected Koorland. He accepted his authority as Lord Commander. For the combined efforts of the Chapters to maintain cohesion, centralised command was needed. Between the traditional calling of the Imperial Fists as the defenders of the Terran wall, and Koorland's status as both a unifier of Successors and a warrior without a Chapter, he was the logical, least objectionable choice for that position.

Adnachiel also accepted the reasons for the Deathwatch. He supported the action. He expected the battle-brothers he had seconded to the kill-teams to commit fully to the effort, and to the cooperation with warriors from other Chapters, no matter what Chapters they might be.

He accepted all the necessities of the struggle against the Beast. Even so, he preferred Koorland to be in a position where Adnachiel had some control over the information he received. The *Herald of Night* was the necessary ship to make the run to the attack moon. It was not necessary that there be any presence on its bridge that was not a Dark Angel.

There were no visual feeds to the Thunderhawk, but Adnachiel ensured Koorland had a channel to the command vox and received a constant update of ship positions relative to the *Herald*. He would know the state of the battle. He would know when the moment came for the launches.

The strike cruiser cut through the void, closing in on the burning region of the attack moon.

'The Imperial Navy still has the orks contained,' Shipmaster Aelia said.

Adnachiel grunted. 'They're holding them only because this is the greatest concentration of ships to destroy,' he said.

The tacticarium screens flickered as they adjusted to the constant changes. The positions of Navy vessels changed slowly compared to the darting swarm of ork ships. Their status changed far more quickly. Green icons flashed amber, then red, then vanished. The frigates and destroyers that made up the blockade fleet were far from being the largest at the Navy's command, but each was still over a kilometre long, with crews numbering in the tens of thousands. The pace at which they were disappearing from the sight of the *Herald*'s auspex array was disturbing. The orks were

feasting on the Terran fleet. There were fifteen destroyers, almost as many frigates, and scores of escorts still in the fighting. Nowhere near enough.

Adnachiel had to hope they would feast a little longer. He resented the necessity for that hope. His anger spurred his determination to see the moon destroyed.

He looked back and forth between the screen readouts and the cloud of battle visible in the oculus. A battle cluster was forming, growing tighter. The Imperial ships were converging as they sought to provide supporting fire for each other. The orks battened on the higher concentration of prey. The blockade still surrounded the moon, but as the Navy fell, gaps opened. The orks were not coming through them yet, but instead they appeared to be intent on the total annihilation of the blockade.

'Commander, we have a possible course plotted,' Aelia said.

'Show me,' Adnachiel said.

The mortal pressed a key on her command throne stationed just below Adnachiel's pulpit. An arcing path appeared on the oculus, cutting through one of the gaps to bring the *Herald of Night* close to the surface of the ork base.

'No,' Adnachiel said. 'The target is the interior.' The nearest approach of Aelia's route would force the kill-teams to breach a surface thick enough to be a planetary crust, or travel to the open maw. That would take too long, giving the orks too much time to detect and counter the attack. 'The jaws are our goal.'

Ork interceptors still streamed from the vast launch bay. The grotesque mouth opened and closed in an imitation of speech. It was the Beast's shout given visual form. It gaped wide, narrowed, then gaped again. It never shut completely.

'Use the gap between the vessels,' Adnachiel said. 'Enter the battle by that path, then cut through to the maw. Maximum speed, continuous fire.'

'So ordered,' said Aelia.

The *Herald of Night* plunged towards the war. It was larger and more powerful than any ship still in the battle, and its approach altered the gravitational tides of conflict. Adnachiel tracked the readings and the oculus display. In his mind's eye, he saw the full shape of the struggle. He saw the shifting currents, the networks of fire, the ripple effects of actions large and small. The cloud began to bulge towards the *Herald.* The movement was slow. The orks were becoming aware of what was closing in, but they were already engaged. The reinforcements coming from the moon turned in the direction of the strike cruiser. Some were destroyed by crossfire within moments of their emergence. Others became caught in the maelstrom of the war. Still others kept their heading.

'The enemy has seen us,' Aelia said.

'And I see them,' Adnachiel answered. 'Maintain course. We will meet them and crush them.'

The strike cruiser entered the gap. To port and starboard, above and below the course of the ship, the void burned and screamed. The edges of the oculus flashed with lance and torpedo fire. Ignited plasma billowed towards the centre of Adnachiel's vision. In the upper right of his view, a dozen ork interceptors dived towards the core of the destroyer *Unstinting.* Its void shields fell. Its hull, already compromised, erupted. A new star burst from the centre. Destroyer and interceptors vanished in its roiling embrace. Edging in from the left was an intersecting web of fire between two frigates as they struggled to cut down the horde of greenskin ships that circled them like feasting insects.

The gap between the battles had looked like empty void from a distance. Now it revealed itself to be a graveyard of broken hulks and dying gas flares. It was dense with ruin. The *Herald of Night* struck the corpses of ships with its prow. A huge tomb of ragged metal half a kilometre long tumbled end-over-end along the *Herald*'s length towards the super-structure. The void shields strained under the impacts, but held. Adnachiel saw the ruin fill the oculus, then vanish as the feed redirected to sensors on the other side of the obstacle.

The hulk slammed against the superstructure. The impact reverberated through the hull. Adnachiel felt it in the walls of the bridge and in the deck. The *Herald of Night* was moving fast, and the mass of the hulk was huge. The first red icons of damage reports appeared on the tacticarium screens.

'Anomalous gravity readings,' Aelia announced. At the same moment, strange waves swept through the ship and Adnachiel felt himself weighed down, then pulled upward as if he might fly to the dome of the bridge. Conflicting forces pressed against him. His Lyman's ear resisted the disorientation, but still his sense of the vertical fragmented. It spun. He held steady. Below, officers and serfs lost their balance. Some fell from their seats. Servitors jerked upward and then down against banks of consoles. The hull groaned.

Adnachiel saw new meaning in the shape of the path. The orks' gravity weapon had swept through these coordinates, a scythe for ships. The reports reaching Terra from the battle had indicated it was active, but in a limited fashion. Its area of effect was narrow. Its strikes were sporadic.

The orks were back, but the injury inflicted on them before was real, Adnachiel thought. The base was weaker.

The *Herald of Night*'s run was a wager. There was no pretending otherwise. But if the aftershocks of the weapon were still being felt, it had been used very recently. Adnachiel disliked wagers. War had too much chance in it already. To willingly engage with it was a form of moral carelessness. His hand was forced, though. And everything about the Deathwatch mission was a wager.

But the fading gravity effects were promising. If he must wager, perhaps he was making a good one. The *Herald of Night* ploughed onward through the debris field, speed undiminished. Ahead, Adnachiel saw a path to the curve of the attack moon's surface. 'Hard to port,' he ordered. 'Fire at will.'

'Hard to port,' Aelia confirmed.

The *Herald*'s bow turned from the darkened path towards the cloud of lethal light, and its batteries acquired targets and fired. The first ork interceptors came into range and died. The hull shook as the ship entered a zone of overlapping shockwaves. Hostile targets closed in.

'Master of the Vox,' Adnachiel called, 'begin a broadcast to all Imperial vessels.'

'Transmitting,' Master of the Vox Enger confirmed.

'Ships of the Imperial Navy,' Adnachiel said. 'We come to

drive a blade through the heart of the greenskins. Hold the xenos. Do not allow them to deflect the blow.' He paused. 'End vox-cast,' he told Enger.

Now the surviving officers of the blockade knew their situation. The *Herald of Night* had not come to reinforce them. Instead, their role was to support its mission.

If any still lived at the end of this day, they would receive the gratitude of the Imperium for their service.

The view in the oculus shifted, reflecting the changes to the *Herald of Night*'s course. The orb of the attack moon moved to the centre. It was partially obscured by the explosions of ships and the pinprick flashes of guns. Its maw snarled, hate made of stone and iron. The base grew larger.

'How close...' Aelia began.

'As close as we are able,' Adnachiel said. He shifted his stance in the pulpit, bracing for the inevitable lash of the gravity weapon, balancing risks, riding the lethal edge of the wager. If the *Herald of Night* took the full force of what the orks were capable of, the mission would end before it had begun. But he had to get the Deathwatch into proximity with the target.

'Get us in a direct line with the jaws,' Adnachiel said. If the gravity weapon fired, the orks would destroy all the ships they were launching. He did not think they would use it unless desperate. The war was still running their way. The blockade was coming apart like the rotten wall it was.

More and more interceptors closed in. The *Herald*'s batteries could not take them all down – they were fast. Their construction seemed crude, brutal shapes hurtling through the void, and they were not agile, but they absorbed more damage than Imperial ships of comparable size. They came at the strike cruiser with the murderous intent of guided meteors.

The *Herald* had left the false calm of the gap for the heart of the storm. Vast engines of destruction warred with machines of shrieking speed. Death lashed out over distances of tens of thousands of kilometres. The strike cruiser became the centre of gravity of the conflict. Ork and Imperial ships converged in response to its movements, and leviathans and lightning found a single focus. The space of the battle constricted.

Beam weapons and torpedoes slammed into the *Herald*. Crippled ork fighters hurled themselves against its shields as they died. In the oculus, the void became a strobing storm of explosions and energy discharges. The void shields rippled and flashed, red and searing violet.

The attack moon was huge. Its circumference surpassed the edges of the oculus.

'Lord Commander Koorland,' Adnachiel voxed. 'Are you ready to launch?'

'We are.'

'Opening bay doors.'

Adnachiel stared straight ahead, at the void and the gaping rage of the target. In the corner of his eye, he saw the multiplying red of damage icons. He ignored them. He felt each shake and tremor of the ship as a personal blow. He stood fast, willing his ship forward. He knew its injuries. Let it know his determination.

The jaws were opening again. The interior of the ork moon filled the centre of the oculus. Adnachiel glared at the hunger of fire and darkness.

'Launch!' he shouted. 'Launch!'

One more klaxon added its voice to the cacophony of warnings on the bridge. It was the only sign of the departure of the Thunderhawks until Koorland spoke again.

'You have taken us to the threshold, brother,' he said. 'Now we have crossed it.'

'Strike hard.'

'The orks will feel our blow even on Ullanor.'

'Bow up!' Adnachiel roared. 'Take us over the pole.' He would make the orks pursue the prize of the *Herald of Night*. He would be their target. He would draw their eyes away from the insignificant ships flying into the moon.

Strike hard, he thought again. Strike hard.

FOUR

The ork attack moon

The three Thunderhawks flew into the maw. They came in low, beneath the flights of the ork fighters, and close to the port side of the jaws. They entered the throat of the monster, a colossal shaft reaching straight down to the centre of the moon. Energy flashed outside the viewing blocks as they crossed the threshold.

Inside the *Reclaimed Honour*, the Ultramarine Simmias said, 'Some form of containment field. They're maintaining their atmosphere.'

'You're impressed,' said Koorland.

'I am respectful of an opponent's capabilities,' the Tech-marine said. 'Doing less would lead to faulty theoreticals and disastrous practicals in battle.'

'And what do you deduce that we don't already know?' Hakon Icegrip asked. The Space Wolf had not donned his helmet yet, and the low snarl of his breathing was audible in the hold. He was taut with impatience.

'I deduce that all aspects of this base are receiving large

amounts of power,' Simmias said, unmoved by the challenge in Icegrip's question. 'Theoretical – much of the damage we inflicted before has been repaired, at least in terms of tactical effects. That is a lot of energy to devote to the preservation of atmosphere in a launch shaft.'

The *Honour* shook. Proximity warnings sounded. Koorland looked through the viewing block. The Thunderhawk was flying so close to the inner wall that it had clipped protruding scaffolding. The walls were crude, uneven, and they whipped by at such speed there could be no evading minor obstacles. The three gunships were travelling through thickets of ragged ends of iron and rock. They were not taking fire yet. Koorland dared to hope they had entered undetected.

'What do you think, Simmias?' the Blood Angel Vepar asked, pointing to the teleport homer on the Techmarine's back. 'Will it work?'

'I can't say. Too much of this technology is unfamiliar.'

He sounded suspicious. Koorland couldn't blame him. The Imperial device had been modified so heavily it was barely recognisable. It was less bulky than the standard model, but had sprouted a tangle of cables and brass spheres.

'The device is xenos-tainted,' said Hanniel.

Koorland turned to the Dark Angels Librarian. 'Of course it is. And we will use its taint to purge the larger one.'

'While teleporting ourselves back to the *Herald*?' said Icegrip. 'There isn't even a platform.'

'Once powered, the machine will respond to the signal from the ship's teleportation pad,' Simmias said. 'It is the

Herald's device that will call us back, while the ones we place on the moon will send it away. Theoretically.'

'Theoretically,' Vepar repeated.

Koorland glanced at Haas. She had said nothing since the launch from the *Herald of Night*. She stared out the viewing block, her face grim with pain and stony determination as she returned to her prison. As he watched, he saw her jerk, as if in bleak recognition. He didn't think it could be. She had never seen the launch shaft.

Even so, at the same moment, the pilot Nithael voxed, 'Approaching primary target.'

'How close can you get us?' Koorland asked.

'I see a major avenue. It looks clear.'

'Take it.'

The *Reclaimed Honour* slowed. The wall became less of a blur. Its details became clear as the gunship turned into a passageway wide enough for a battalion of tanks. The edges of the opening were broken, as if the tunnel had been cut here by violent action. The kill-team shed grav-harnesses and stood. The Thunderhawk came to a rapid halt, landing with a blast of exhaust nozzles. The forward ramp dropped, and the first of the Deathwatch squads stormed down onto the tunnel floor. Koorland led his squad and Haas off while the gunship lifted off again.

'Good hunting,' said Nithael. 'I will await your return.'

'Fly well, brother,' Koorland told him. He watched the *Honour* turn back towards the shaft. There was a glow coming from it, dark and red illumination from the engines of the passing interceptors still heading out to fight the blockade. The other two Thunderhawks should be finding their landing targets very soon. The *Reclaimed Honour*'s departure was a good omen. Perhaps all three would exit the moon and return to the *Herald of Night*.

Perhaps this mission was not completely mad.

The tunnel they were in was almost wholly dark. A few guttering lumen globes dangled from cables. They were widely spaced. Between them hung the broken husks of many others.

'This region is no longer used,' Simmias said. He gestured at the cables. 'There is illumination here by chance, not design. The power is going everywhere, even where it is no longer needed.'

'But what was this used for?' said Vepar. 'Wherever it begins, it leads only to the shaft. What use is that for vehicles?'

'The tunnel is for construction,' Haas answered. 'They build fast. The big passages allow them to mobilise quickly.'

'Indeed,' said Koorland. 'Look how quickly they rebuilt after our attack.' To Haas, he said, 'There have likely been considerable changes. We have an approximate location on the auspex. Do you think you can take us there?'

'I haven't been there, but I can show you the best way to get around.' She moved further along the tunnel, sticking to the right-hand wall. 'Here,' she said, pointing up.

There was an opening just below her head height on the wall. Haas reached up and pulled herself inside. Koorland and the others followed. It was just large enough for a Space Marine to walk in a crouch. There was no light here at all, though Koorland's helm lamp picked out more tangles of cables and conduits on the low ceiling of the passageway.

'I've seen the little creatures use these,' she said. 'There's room for many of them, and these shafts keep them out of the way of the large orks.'

'Vermin,' said Icegrip.

'Cunning vermin,' Hanniel answered. 'They will need to be silenced quickly. The point is not to bring the full horde down on us. We are coming as a shadow among the greenskins.'

The Space Wolf grunted, acquiescing. 'A shadow with teeth,' he said.

Koorland showed Haas the auspex. The readings were marked by numerous power surges. Three were singled out – two were close together, one much larger than the other. The energy source furthest away was the known quantity. It fluctuated moment to moment, winking out of existence then becoming explosively bright, more intense than any other signal on the screen. It was the gate. The orks had reopened it. The third kill-team would close it again, this time forever.

The other two targets were the ones whose locations were approximate guesses, reached through a combination of analysis of power signatures and Haas' memories of her imprisonment. Koorland pointed to the larger of the two clustered targets. This, he hoped, was the attack moon's power source. 'Can you find the way?' he asked.

'I think so. I only saw it once. But there is a kind of order to the pathways here. Things flow to and from that location.'

'Show us, then,' said Koorland.

The shadows with teeth moved off.

* * *

The *Penitent Wrath* dropped Thane's squad on a rough platform just outside a tunnel so ragged it would have seemed natural if the walls had not been made of patched-together stone and iron. The five Space Marines entered the crevice. It made a sharp turn almost immediately, then another, its path nothing more than a fault line between walls. Within seconds, the squad vanished from sight of the launch shaft.

The passageway angled left, then dropped down, and kept sloping downward.

'This is taking us in the wrong direction,' Asger Warfist said.

'I know,' said Thane. The extrapolated target was a control complex, located above the presumed power source. The mission was already riddled with uncertainty and guesswork. Moving down and away from the goal only added to the frustration. Thane played his helm lamp over the walls ahead, looking for any kind of exit.

'There,' said Abathar.

Thane stopped and looked up at the spot the Dark Angels Techmarine had isolated. Twenty metres up, where the sloping walls of the tunnel almost met, two openings faced each other.

'No bridge,' said Straton, the Ultramarine. 'Do the greenskins leap over the gap in the dark?'

'I suggest this passage is a result of a shift in the walls,' Abathar said. 'That tunnel is not likely to be still in use.'

'I think you're right,' said Forcas. The Blood Angels Librarian pointed to a spot on the floor of the fissure, directly below the broken tunnel. Three ork bodies lay broken, smashed open against the raised, jagged edges of metal plating.

'How do we get up there?' Straton asked.

Thane watched Abathar examine the right-hand wall. Its surface was rough, a contusion of folds and cracks. He fired up the plasma cutter on his right servo-arm and played it against the wall. The light stabbed at the eyes in the gloom. It took only a few seconds for the cutter to melt through the stone and metal and form a rough handhold. Abathar looked at his handiwork, then back upward. 'The lean of the wall is unfortunate, but acceptable. We can climb.' He raised the servo-arm and burned another ledge into the wall.

It took ten minutes for Abathar to cut a ladder all the way to the top. Once inside the tunnel, Thane found the path hewing much more closely to the desired heading. Warfist strode at his side. Though he wore his helm, Thane could sense the Space Wolf's impatience for battle in the quick jerks of his movements. He was holding himself back, though, and Thane noticed him checking on the movements of the rest of the squad, especially Abathar, weighed down by the cumbersome teleport homer. Given the history of tension between the Dark Angels and the Space Wolves, Thane was pleased to see this automatic gesture on the part of Warfist. It made the black of the Space Marines' armour more than a gesture. They were functioning as a team.

The creation of the Deathwatch livery had struck a resonant chord in Thane's soul. He had seen an echo of the formation of the Last Wall. But that had been the coming together of Chapters who were all sons of Dorn. The Deathwatch was something else again. He did not know if it was more profound, or more meaningful. He did not try to guess at its consequences, though he knew they would be real,

and far-reaching. He had pondered whether he too would change the colour of his armour. He had decided against it. He was part of the Last Wall, and its continued existence was necessary. It was about more than victory. It was about rebuilding.

The Deathwatch, he thought, was both simpler and more complex. It was the forging together of forces so disparate, in some cases so alien to each other, that loyalty to the Emperor was the only common bond. It did not exist to build, Thane thought. Not in the same sense as the Last Wall. But as he travelled the darkness of the attack moon, the colours of his own armour almost as shadowy here as the black of his squad, he was part of the Deathwatch blade. We do not stand guard, he thought. We are not the sentinels on the rampart.

We watch only to find the moment to strike. We are destruction.

They reached an intersection. The tunnel split into five paths. Thane stopped and consulted the auspex. The energy reading was to the left of their position, and two of the paths looked promising. All had cables running down them.

Since disembarking from the *Penitent Wrath*, Thane had heard the heartbeat of the attack moon. It was as deep and hard as a continent, irregular in its rhythm yet colossal in its strength. It had grown much louder since they left the crevice, booming now down all the tunnels. Dust shook from the roof of the passageway. There were other sounds too – a clamour of bestial snarling, the clangs of heavy blows, the high-pitched squeals of the vermin-like creatures that swarmed in menial servility around the feet of the orks.

'We should wait,' Straton said.

'For what?' Warfist asked, his patience stretching taut.

'A frequency of traffic might point us to the correct route.'

'That's leaving things to chance at best,' Warfist scoffed. 'And wait how long? The success of the other two operations depends on us.'

'Five minutes,' Thane said.

Two minutes passed. Koorland's voice came over Thane's helm vox. 'Squad Gladius, this is Sword. What is your status?'

'Still searching.'

'We have found the power source. Awaiting your action.'

'Understood. What about the gate?'

'Squad Crozius is also in position.'

'We will take the target shortly.' He vowed they would, if he had to punch his way through the interior walls of the moon.

'Good. The Emperor protects.'

'The Emperor protects.'

In the fourth minute, brutish voices sounded closer in the far left passageway. Thane held up an arm, waiting a few seconds more. The noises came closer. The other paths were silent. Warfist was right – Straton's surmise was barely more than a guess. But the direction of the tunnel was correct, and there was little else to go on.

The bobbing glow of portable lamps appeared in the tunnel.

Thane lowered his arm.

Warfist shot forward, fists tight, arms extended, lightning claws at the ready. Thane and Straton followed, each with

gladius drawn. The kills had to be silent. Forcas and Aba-thar brought up the rear.

Warfist rounded a curve in the tunnel. The voices became snarls of alarm. As Thane reached the curve, a shout was cut off, turning into a wet gurgle. He heard a sound like heavy bags of meat slapping against rock.

He made the turn. Warfist was in the centre of a group of about a dozen orks. Two lay dead. He had plunged into the centre of the greenskins and was fighting the largest. It was taller than Warfist, its head brushing against the roof of the tunnel. A huge wound gaped in its throat and its jaws were wide in near-silent, choking fury. It swung a massive ham-mer at the Space Wolf. Warfist jabbed with his left claws, sinking them deep into the greenskin's arm at the elbow. He twisted. The greenskin's hand opened, nerveless, and the hammer fell to the tunnel floor. A second later, so did the ork's lower arm.

The other orks charged the kill-team. Thane pulled back his blade, then struck forward with servo-aided force. The gladius stabbed all the way through his target's throat and out of the back of its neck. Thane slashed sideways. The ork's head, half-severed, lolled back. Blood geysered; the body fell. Thane leapt over it and grasped another ork by the face. The beast jerked back in surprise and Thane yanked it forward. The greenskin chopped futilely at his armour with a heavy cleaver before Thane rammed the gladius into its chest. He angled the blow upward, drove the blade higher, cutting through gut and heart.

Beside him, Straton took down two more orks in swift, cold, precise strikes. A handful of others were still rushing forward. They were snarling in rage, and in their fury they were not shouting in alarm. Anger was the norm among orks. Even if those snarls reached others, they would not pay attention as they would to a summons.

Abathar's plasma cutter burned through a pair of skulls. Warfist gutted the giant and turned back to impale the last of the attacking greenskins through the spine. That left the smaller, scuttling creatures. Their squeals were drowned out by the snarls of their masters. They fled, scrambling over the corpse of the monster, fast in their panic. Just a few metres ahead, Thane saw what looked like burrows in the stone. If the tiny xenos reached those holes, they would be impossible to follow. He reached for his boltgun, willing to risk the noise of concussion blasts.

Forcas stepped forward, right hand outstretched, energy crackling from his psychic hood and down his arm. Lightning flashed from his fingertips and struck the vermin, searing them to ash. There was a sharp crack of thunder. The smell of burned ozone filled the tunnel. The air rippled with the after-effects of dissipating warp power. Warfist's wolf-headed helm turned from the smoking remains of the creatures towards Forcas. If he was disgusted by the Blood Angel's sorcery, he refrained from saying so.

'We have gained some time,' Straton said. 'But we have little to spare.'

'Agreed,' said Thane.

They moved quickly down the corridor. The pounding of machines and the violent discharge of energy grew louder, covering the sound of their boots as they ran. The tunnel twisted, then came to a stop.

It opened into a huge cavern. From this position, Thane could see only a small portion of its upper reaches. Ahead was a rough metal ramp leading up to what appeared to be a massive promontory that jutted out into the space of the cavern. At the top of the promontory was a roofless structure. The tops of its walls were angular, as if it were a jagged iron crown and energy coils rose from the corners, leaning out over the void. Innumerable cables ran from the base of the structure and into the air below the promontory, or down its slope into other tunnels opening up on the wall along its base. Some were as thick as Land Raiders. Searing light flashed from inside the structure. Energy arced and snapped from the coils, and the booms of the discharges were deafening.

In the gaps in the walls, figures moved back and forth, silhouetted by the pulsing light within. They were large. Their forms were strange, built up with something artificial that had the wrong shape for armour.

There was activity up and down the ramp as hordes of the tiny greenskins hauled wagons of equipment up, and burned-out debris back down. The creatures were urged to greater efforts by orks wielding shock prods.

'A clear run to the top,' Warfist said over the vox.

Thane eyed the traffic on the ramp and agreed. These orks were not a serious obstacle. 'The alarm will be raised,' he warned. 'Our time will be limited.'

'What time we have will depend on Squad Crozius,' said Straton.

'The timing of all three squads is critical,' Forcas said. 'We must have faith in them, and they in us.'

'For Terra and the Emperor, then,' said Thane. 'For the Deathwatch!'

'For the Deathwatch!' the squad shouted, voices amplified by vox-casters.

Warriors in black stormed out of the tunnel and up the ramp, into the rising shriek of orks.

'Ingenious,' said the Blood Angels Techmarine Gadreel. 'Despite the damage the Last Wall inflicted, the orks have managed to amplify the power of what remained.'

'I have had more than enough of their ingenuity,' said Iairos.

The Ultramarines sergeant had led Squad Crozius to a small tunnel that ended three metres up from the floor of the gate chamber. Based on the reports of the first engagement, a large portion of the cavern must have fallen in. It was still well over a kilometre wide, but to the right of the kill-team's position was a massive collapse. It looked as if a mountain had fallen on the machinery that powered the gate.

Where there had been three Titan-sized horns, now there was only one, a monstrous patchwork that appeared to have been assembled from the wreckage of the previous three. Its balance was precarious, its upper half thicker than the lower, and its peak was a colossal, trifurcated claw. Countless support chains now ran from the horn to the walls and slope of rubble. The horn trembled and vibrated from the energies fed to it and summoned by it. Eldritch light exploded and imploded in the centre of the claw. Every time the burning force collapsed in on itself, there was a

cave-filling flash on the platform at its base, and another war party of orks appeared.

'There is our primary target,' said Gadreel. He pointed.

To the left of the tunnel, an enormous power cable six metres thick entered the cavern. A short way to the right, it split into myriad smaller cables, running power to the hulking machines that, in turn, provided energy and direction to the functioning of the gate.

'They are vulnerable,' said Valtar Skyclaw. The Space Wolf Rune Priest looked up at the horn. 'The unclean energies here are on the cusp of overwhelming their material constraints. We will destroy this gate forever.'

'Not until we claim its power source,' Gadreel said.

'Aye,' Skyclaw admitted.

'Where is Gladius?' the Dark Angel Vehuel asked.

'Nearly in position,' Iairos said. Until the power was shut off temporarily, they could not attempt to splice into the main cable and link it to Gadreel's teleport homer.

'How long will it take to cut into that?' asked Eligos, the second Blood Angel.

'Not long,' said Gadreel.

'Attacking control centre,' Thane called over the vox. 'Stand by. Stand by.'

Time accelerated and slowed at once. With Thane's call, the mission entered the narrow window of success. The timing of the actions required from all three squads came down to a matter of seconds. Sword and Crozius could not take their targets until the power flow was under the control of Gladius. Thane's squad would not be able to hold their position if Crozius did not stop the reinforcements from arriving. Crozius could not risk destroying the gate without also destroying its teleport homer.

The allotment of seconds crawled as Iairos took in the variables of the battlefield. He saw the vectors of action and their possible consequences. He waited, forced to guess at the moment and duration of Thane's success.

So many unknowns.

Theoretical: action must be predicated on the known skill of allies.

Practical: attack at the opportune moment based on the presumption of skill.

He gave Thane a few more precious seconds.

Then he leapt from the tunnel, leading Squad Crozius towards the main cable's junction.

The moon's power plant was the size of a city. The cavern was so huge that Koorland could not make out the far walls. Haas brought Sword to an entrance on the floor of the cave. Her sense of how the shafts worked had been accurate, and the squad had moved quickly. They had encountered a few groups, quickly despatched, of the dwarfish greenskins.

Now the Deathwatch was surrounded by generators larger than hab-blocks. They were hulking machines, squat despite their height. It was impossible to see more than a few hundred metres in any direction. The generators sat at all angles on the cavern floor. The paths running between them were wide, but never straight for more than a few dozen metres.

A tangled forest of cables ran between the generators. They trembled and convulsed with surges. Sparks flew from flawed junctions and haloes of lightning crackled down their lengths. The din was immense, a deep, continuous tremor that vibrated deep in Koorland's chest. The sound was so thick, it tried to stop his hearing. The sharp snap of energy cut through the tremor with a searing arrhythmia. The cavern rumbled and shrieked with the roars of beasts and the hiss of serpents. It rang with the endless, grating choir of xenos industry.

'There is the power of a small sun here,' Simmias said as they paused at the entrance. 'We cannot cut in blindly.'

'And we come to steal this energy, not to destroy it,' said Koorland.

In the flashing gloom, orks clambered up and down the generators. The energy production was so violent, every few moments Koorland saw an electrocuted greenskin tumble from the heights of the machines.

'There are so many generators,' Vepar said. 'How can we let Gladius know which node to shut down for us?'

'We take the nearest,' Simmias said. 'Damage it, but do not destroy it.'

Vepar turned to the Ultramarine. 'That smacks of messy improvisation.'

'There is no perfection in this situation,' Simmias told him. 'The practical is constructed from the necessary.'

'Improvisation, in other words,' Vepar said. Koorland thought there was a glint of amusement in his tone.

Thane's declaration of war came through the vox. 'We go now!' Koorland shouted.

Squad Sword raced towards the nearest generator. The labouring orks saw the Space Marines and Haas and roared in surprise and rage. From the ground and from the scaffolding of the generators, they opened fire. The rain of bullets was disorganised. The aim was wild.

Hakon Icegrip took the lead of the charge, ripping through orks with frost blade and bolt pistol. He howled as he ran, the fury of his voice a terrifying, distorted rasp from his vox-casters, a monstrous cry at once animal and machine. The squealing orklings fled before him. Icegrip gave their masters no time to respond. He ploughed through an explosion of blood and flesh.

Haas was not far behind him. She sprinted from enemy to enemy, her shock maul at full power, its blows immobilising and burning the orks before she finished them with autopistol rounds to their skulls. She was shouting, but Koorland could make out no words. Her cries were a pure expression of vengeance and rage. She had returned to the moon to avenge a defeat, and to purge her nightmares of the billions dead.

Vepar moved in tandem with Koorland. The Blood Angel used his bolter, cutting down orks that tried to close in on the flanks of Icegrip and Haas. Vepar fired in precise short bursts. Every pull of the trigger counted. Where he looked, greenskin heads burst apart. There was a careful art to his kills, a restrained wrath channelled into a perfection of aim, as if something worse were held in check by the force of discipline. Hanniel and Simmias followed at a more measured pace. They were no less destructive, their bolter fire systematic.

The run from the tunnel to the generator covered hundreds of metres in a single, relentless burst of speed. As the squad approached the huge device, Simmias' fire turned from the orks to the generator. He shot at the junction points on the near facade, blowing away cables. They fell, lashing back and forth. Hanniel reached out for the orks on the scaffolding. An eldritch storm bellowed over the generator, wher two lightnings entwined and fought, the warp against the materium. Orks screamed, incinerated by the warring forces, their corpses dropping, falling to ash before they reached the ground. The generator was enveloped in coruscating power.

The kill-team reached the base of the generator, tore through its defenders, then rounded a corner. Ahead was a cable twice Koorland's height.

'There,' said Simmias. 'That one.'

'Thane,' Koorland voxed. 'We have our target. Do you see it? Shut it down!'

The ork engineers were ready for Gladius. Thane and Warfist burst across the threshold first. Three engineers faced them. They were large beasts, made even larger by the harnesses they wore. Power coils and portable generators rose from the greenskins' shoulders and backs like the arcing spines of saurians. The air around them shimmered. Static broke out across Thane's auto-senses as they reacted to an overload of energy. He had trouble focusing on the targets. Their image juddered, a cracking mosaic, and his lenses fought to stabilise. He paused and fired. His shells exploded on contact with the orks' force fields.

Warfist snarled with frustration and rage. He hurled himself at the nearest engineer and the force field flared from the impact of the lightning claws, then collapsed with a deafening concussion. Warfist grappled with the ork. It struck him with a heavy tool that resembled a fusion of a shock maul and a plasma cutter. Electricity and flame washed over the Space Wolf's armour.

The other two orks came at Thane with similar weapons. He maglocked his boltgun and raised his chainsword, throwing himself at the closest ork, using his mass and velocity against the barrier of the shield. He felt the resistance as an invisible force that pushed against him and stabbed through his armour and his body with powerful jolts. A vibrating numbness suffused his limbs. He pushed on, the chainsword sparking and shrieking. There was a blast, and his blade moved quickly again. He brought it down on the ork's skull and cut it in half before it could hit him with its weapon.

Warfist punched through the shocks and flame and jammed his lightning claws through his opponent's throat. Before the third ork could attack either Space Marine, Abathar entered the control centre and hit the beast with his power axe. Two energy fields collided. The interior of the centre blazed with their fury, then the axe blade broke through. It severed the largest of the ork's energy coils. The harness exploded, consuming the ork and hurling Abathar back out of the entrance. He was back in the next breath.

Outside, Forcas and Straton held off the orks seeking to retake the centre. The speed of the counter-attack did not concern Thane. He had expected such a response as soon as Gladius had attacked. What worried him was its strength. The orks already numbered more than a hundred. The choke point of the ramp and the lack of shelter gave the

Deathwatch an advantage, but two defenders would not be able to hold off the horde for long. Warfist lunged out of the doorway to join them.

Koorland's report came over the vox.

'Sword is ready,' Thane told Abathar. The Techmarine nodded and approached the control surfaces of the centre. They were crude and massive, like everything else fashioned by orkish hands, but Thane regarded them with more wariness than contempt. The power the orks wielded belied the rough construction.

There is technology here that is beyond our own, he reminded himself. The controls were a conglomeration of huge, clumsy levers, switches and buttons. They flashed with bursts of energy. Thane could not tell if the flares were overloads, short circuits, or if they were deliberate. Since the giant coils at each corner of the centre gave off so much excess, it was as if the centre were caught in a perpetual storm. Thane had no way to guess if the small blasts from the controls were by design or not.

Beyond the control surfaces, there was no wall. The centre was perched on the very edge of the promontory. Thane had a perspective of the entire power plant, of kilometres of colossal, linked generators. From this height, he felt as if he were looking into a cauldron of lightning. He could see no order to the construction. It seemed to be haphazard, machines piled atop machines, connections as superfluous as they were dangerous.

How were these beings a threat? he wondered. How had they not destroyed themselves? How could any of this work? How had it not blown up the instant it was activated?

The questions multiplied, though he knew there would be no answers. The Mechanicus might know them. Perhaps not. The answers did not matter. The action did.

Seconds had passed since the death of the ork engineers. Thane contained his impatience as Abathar examined the controls. The seconds were precious. Yet a mistake would be catastrophic.

Abathar was cautious. His helmet moved back and forth as he scanned the controls. He touched nothing, though Thane sensed the speed of his evaluation. After a few moments, his attention focused on a section of the controls to the far left. He looked back and forth between the cavern and the technological jumble before him. 'There,' he said. He pointed to flames at the extreme left of the cavern. 'That is a true fire.'

Thane looked. Abathar was right. The flickering light also suggested flames close to the ground. All the other flashes Thane could see came from no lower than the cables, midway up the flanks of the generators.

'A generator in distress,' Abathar said. He moved his hand to a switch. Just above it, sparks flew with a surprisingly steady rhythm. 'That,' the Dark Angel said, 'is what passes for a remote alarm with these brutes.'

'You're sure?'

'As sure as I must be.' He flipped the switch.

The sparks ceased. Exposed wiring glowed red, then went dark.

'Sword, this is Gladius,' Thane voxed. 'We believe we have cut the power to your generator. Please confirm.'

'Confirmed,' Koorland said after a moment. 'Splicing in.'

Thane turned to Abathar. 'And the gate?' he asked.

The Techmarine had already moved to the other end of the control banks. 'The machines grow brighter towards the right,' he said. 'There is a higher intensity of power gathering there. We must seek the greatest current.'

Thane looked off to the right, following the pattern of light. The flares converged at a blinding point that pulsed in and out of existence. 'I see it,' he said.

'As do I.'

'But it is not damaged.'

'There appears to be a rough concordance between the position of the generators and their controls here. A crude organisation, perfect for these brutes.'

These brutes who perform wonders we cannot hope to emulate, Thane thought. Even so, Abathar's logic was sound. The orks combined brutishness and ingenuity in a manner that defied comprehension. It was necessary simply to accept the fusion and attempt to counter its effects.

Abathar wrapped his gauntlet around a lever the size of a bolter. He nodded at Thane.

'Crozius,' Thane voxed, 'we are attempting to cut the power to the gate.'

'We are ready,' said Iairos.

Abathar pulled the lever. It moved with a foul metallic grinding, as if the end of the shaft went all the way to the core of the attack moon. An ear-shattering klaxon sounded. Scores of crackling warning flares shot up from the consoles around the lever.

'You have angered the ork machines,' said Thane.

'Good.'

In the distance, the searing point dimmed to an ember, then went out.

'The gate is closed!' Iairos shouted, triumphant. 'The gate is closed!'

Thane grinned. He imagined he could hear a howl coming from the throat of every ork on the moon as their device ceased to respond to their commands. He checked the clip on his bolter. 'Now we wait on the others,' he said.

'I'm sure you can convince the orks to have patience,' said Abathar. He unshouldered the teleport homer and extended its mechadendrites. His servo-arm's plasma cutter sliced open a portion of the control surface, exposing a madness that Thane could barely qualify as technological. Abathar began linking the homer to the madness.

'On what basis can we expect that to work?' Thane asked.

'On faith,' Abathar answered. 'The Mechanicus has made this a human device, but the taint of the xenos remains. On this day, that taint is necessary. It will permit the union of the homer to the greenskin network.'

'Then you have my faith and my hope,' Thane said. 'The Emperor protects.'

'The Emperor protects.'

Thane clapped Abathar on the pauldron and made for the door.

Outside the control centre, a green wave surged towards the ramp.

Iairos fired his bolter in a wide, repeating arc. Greenskin chests and skulls burst apart. Bodies fell on bodies. A mound of corpses grew. He timed his kills carefully. Theoretical:

each foe killed at the right moment becomes a new obstacle to the others. Already he had created a protective wall of flesh taller than a man, blocking the left-hand and forward approaches to Squad Crozius' position.

Behind him, Gadreel had cut into the housing of the giant cable. Where it began its branching into the smaller lines, he was connecting the mechadendrites of the modified teleport homer. The device would draw upon multiple branches of power.

'How long?' Iairos called out.

'Nearly there.'

On the right, Vehuel and Eligos added to the wall of bodies. Skyclaw stood atop the mound, the centre of a shrieking storm. Winds flattened the orks as they struggled to close with the kill-team. Lightning struck them down when they dared to attack the Rune Priest. His axe blade shone a brilliant, frigid blue. Ice flew on the wind, sharp as steel, lacerating flesh, slashing faces. Orks staggered on the top of the mound, blinded by ice shards. They screamed, holding their eyes. Blood poured from between their fingers. Iairos did not waste shells putting those brutes down. When they came within Skyclaw's reach, he decapitated them with a single, wrathful stroke of his runic axe.

'A grand battle!' Skyclaw shouted. 'Son of Guilliman, you have led us to a rare feast!'

'We will avenge the dead of Ullanor yet,' said Eligos.

'By the will of the Emperor,' Iairos said. Yet he felt the pressure of passing time. The gate was dark, and the orks' attention was divided by the simultaneous attacks on three fronts. The squads were benefiting, Iairos thought, from the uncertainty over which target was the most important, the most vulnerable. The orks were fighting blindly, for the moment without the direction that had made them so lethal on Ullanor. But the confusion would pass, and they were still mustering ever greater numbers of reinforcements. Greenskins poured out of every tunnel entrance. They converged on Crozius at a run. They died on the near approach.

For now.

Iairos calculated his team was at the edge of what it could hold off. And once Gadreel's task was complete, they would be facing a much greater flood of the enemy.

'Done,' said Gadreel. 'Let us bear witness now to the will of the Omnissiah.'

'Thane,' Iairos voxed. 'Let the current flow.'

The orks were concentrating their fire now. With Sword no longer moving, the attacks were becoming more and more focused and savage. Desperate too, Koorland wanted to believe. He wanted the orks to know doom was rushing for them. He wanted them to know fear. He wanted them to know fate had turned its back on them at last.

Simmias had cut through a slab of the generator's shielding. While he spliced the teleport homer into the inner workings of the machine, Koorland, Vepar and Haas held the ground attacks off. Icegrip had climbed up to the cable network. The lines were thick enough to walk on, and he raced over the network, taking down the ork gunners. Xenos blood rained on the cavern floor. Bodies hailed down upon their kin. Hanniel's warp lighting lashed out again and again, burning more of the greenskins above.

And still the enemy fire became more and more focused. Solid rounds pounded against Koorland's armour. Some of the rounds were large enough, the hits direct enough, to punch through the ceramite. He blinked off the damage warnings. There was no shelter, and nowhere to go until the task was done.

Haas' armour was shattered over her chest and shoulders, though she still had her helmet. She kept moving, dodging from one end of the squad's position to the other. Her shouts had become a raspy snarl. Her breath was pained. Her shots counted, though. She fought with the purpose of a warrior certain of her death, and as certain that she would take the enemy down with her.

'Now!' Simmias shouted.

'Now!' Koorland repeated into the vox. 'Thane! It must be now!'

'Turn the power back on!' Thane voxed to Abathar. The roar of the attacking orks was too great for him to make himself heard otherwise. He did not look back. Standing above Forcas, Straton and Warfist, he sprayed bolter shells down the ramp into the rising tide. The four Space Marines killed the greenskins by the score, but the tide still grew. The orks charged over heaps of bodies. There were thousands of them massing at the base of the ramp, the press of the mob pushing them on. Their horde was so dense, it pushed even the dead forward.

There would be no retreat through the tunnels.

Squad Gladius slowed the orks. Each second was a victory, Thane thought. Each second might be *the* victory.

The orks did not engage in massed fire, wary of destroying the centre they had come to save. If they had, Gladius would have already lost.

There was a huge flash behind Thane. For a moment, the ramp and its combatants were lit in negative colours.

'Power restored,' Abathar reported. 'The devices are charging.'

The gate burst into life. A foul, captive star blazed in the grip of the horn. It vanished, and an emerald explosion on the platform released a mob of heavily armoured orks and a tank into the cavern. The tank had a massive, spiked siege blade. It thundered off the platform in a cloud of black promethium smoke. Its hulking silhouette bristled with guns. Iairos saw it barrel across the cavern floor and knew the mission's strategy had become desperate.

'If they start using heavy armour...' said Vehuel.

'They may be willing to sacrifice what we have seized,' Iairos finished.

The tank's blade struck the wall of bodies. The rampart was taller than a Space Marine now. It toppled forward, a carrion wave. Skyclaw turned towards the vehicle. The storm gathered around him. It surrounded him with a gleaming, whistling shroud of razor ice. He shot his arms forward and the storm screamed with all its concentrated strength into the tank. Ice slashed through every gap in the armour, tore the plating, and shredded the crew. The tank swerved, out of control, but its turrets still barked. A shell slammed into Skyclaw. It hurled him from the remains of the corpse wall. He hit the cavern floor with such force he cracked stone. The storm died.

The Space Wolf's icon blinked an ominous amber in Iairos' helm display.

The tank was still moving. Iairos ran forward, his bolter on full auto-bursts. He held the gun in one hand, and with the other he unclipped a frag grenade. He jumped up the fallen wall, hurling the grenade through a rent in the armour. The cab of the vehicle exploded. Torn bodies flew out of it. The tank rode over the wall and then stopped, a new obstacle.

The gate flashed again. More orks appeared. And more tanks.

A snarl erupted from a vox-caster. It was a sound that began as something vaguely human, rising until it became a monstrous shriek of hunger. It was nothing but need, a drive that was beyond human, beyond animal. At first Iairos thought he was hearing the wolf howl of Skyclaw. But the Space Wolf had not moved.

The sound came from Eligos.

The Blood Angel had left his position to the right of Gadreel. He tore over the ground towards the nearest group of orks. They were racing to finish off Skyclaw, who had risen to his knees. Eligos pounded past the Space Wolf, chainsword drawn, and plunged into the orks, blade roaring. He did not fight as he had before. Gone was the elegant exactitude of his violence. He was worse than a butcher. His blows were savage, careless, lethal. The roaring from the vox-caster cut off as he shed his helmet. His face was contorted. It was a rictus, his teeth bared as if they would devour hunger itself.

Eligos was not rescuing Skyclaw. But his whirlwind of violence blunted the orks' attack long enough for Skyclaw to regain his feet, lift his bolt pistol and shoot back. Iairos and Gadreel rushed to his position. Vehuel moved in more slowly, maintaining a wide field of fire, cutting back at the advance of the horde for another second, and another second.

Iairos stood at Skyclaw's side, blasting at the enemy. Gadreel ran to Eligos. The Techmarine called to his brother, shouting his name over and over. Eligos did not respond. He tore the orks apart. The tide closed in on all of them, a constriction of foul smell, brutal muscle, drooling fangs and misshapen blades. A vibrating chainaxe cut into Iairos' flank. He spun into the hit, firing as he turned. The stream of mass-reactive shells pulped the features of his attacker and the orks on either side.

Gadreel blinded one ork after another with his plasma cutter. He called and called his brother's name in vain. Iairos did not understand the nature of the frenzy that had taken Eligos, but at this stage he almost welcomed it. The Blood Angel fought with such reckless fury he was forcing another small pause on the ork advance.

Iairos stood back to back with Skyclaw, a wall of huge, green brutishness before him. The Rune Priest's breathing on the vox was ragged. The readout of his life signs was still flashing amber.

The teleportation device was still charging. A hum filled the cavern. It was gargantuan. It was in the walls, the floor, the air. The entire moon vibrated. A terrible song was coming into being. Soon it would have a voice.

'A few moments more,' Gadreel voxed. 'A few–'

* * *

Light.

Light of breaking. Of dissolution. Of shattering, of edges, of fragmentation.

The end of here and the end of there. Death of space. Death of time.

Death.

Light of breaking.

Light of breaking.

All bro

       ken.

Koorland gasped. Blood filled his mouth and his lungs. He was standing in the centre of the teleportation platform of the *Herald of Night*. Haas was on her hands and knees, shaking with enough force to fracture bone. All the squads were present. The other Space Marines seemed as unsteady on their feet.

He had never experienced a teleportation like this. He had been ripped into nothing, then reassembled, and every particle of his being remembered the pain of destruction and rebirth. Between the two lay an infinitesimal portion of a second that was as wide as aeons.

The hum was still growing. He could feel it even this far from the moon, through the hull of the strike cruiser.

He commanded his body to move. It obeyed with reluctance. With limbs of crumbling rockcrete, he walked from the teleportation platform. By the time he and his brothers reached the bridge, he could run again.

In the oculus, the moon was still there. The homers had functioned as Kubik had promised. They had locked on to the sensors in the armour and transported the tiny mass of the Deathwatch kill-teams before they had gathered the full power needed to send the ork base out of the sector.

'Why has it not gone?' Haas whispered. Her teeth chattered. She did not yet have control over her body.

'It will. We are victorious.' Koorland said this even as he watched the explosions of the void war. Nothing was finished.

But the teleporters worked. They were working. They had triumphed.

Staring at the moon, Simmias said, 'That is... unexpected...'

The mountains, canyons and plains of the ork base were suffused with a shifting, retina-slashing glow. And they were moving. The mountains rocked back and forth. Peaks collapsed in on themselves. The canyons of iron pulled wide, the crust of the moon tearing like flesh. The plains heaved as if inconceivable leviathans were struggling to the surface.

'What is happening?' said Koorland.

Simmias shook his head. 'The theoreticals of the technology do not account for this. The disassembly of the material body is instantaneous.'

'It didn't feel like it,' said Haas.

'This geomorphic distortion is abnormal.'

'Shipmaster,' Adnachiel said, 'pull us back.'

Simmias said, 'There is no distance we can reach. Our fates have already been decided.'

'The Emperor protects,' said Vepar.

'The Emperor protects,' Koorland repeated. He barely heard his own voice. He watched the vast agony take the moon. He saw dissolution approach.

We have done this to you, he thought. We have ended you. We *are* victorious.

There had been few triumphs in this war. If this was his last one, he would enjoy it.

The end came first as a brilliance that consumed the spectrum. Koorland's lens shutters slammed down, but not fast enough. He saw the absolute light still.

The shutters opened again, and let him see the moon's end. Half the sphere had vanished. What remained looked like a skull cut cleanly along a diagonal line. That form held just long enough for Koorland to understand what he was seeing. Then it erupted.

A swarm of asteroids hurtled through the void. The shattered surface tore through the warring ships.

He had begun coming to the Cerebrium again. Mesring did not let any of the other High Lords know. They did not come because of what they feared to see. They hid from the light of the ork moon under the cracked dome of the Great Chamber.

Mesring came to see the very thing that kept them away. The top of the Widdershins Tower pierced the clouds more often than any other point of the Inner Palace. Mesring was confident of being alone here, and of being able to contemplate the moon.

He saw the flash. Suddenly, there was an impossible shape in the heavens. Then it flew apart.

Mesring gaped. He stared. His mind was blank except for an inchoate horror.

The great light faded. Where the moon had been was a sudden blackness, the return of the void.

Smaller flashes and glints surrounded the absence where the moon had been. Some of the glints grew stronger. They became more consistent. Their number grew.

He understood nothing. He was bearing witness to a transcendent death, and his thought could not encompass it. He stood at the casement, his body numb, all his awareness focused on a point hundreds of thousands of kilometres away.

The points came closer. The glints became shards of white light. Still he did not understand.

He stayed where he was, fear and horror and helpless anger combining in an alchemy of madness.

He was standing there, blank, lost, when the fragments of the moon entered Terra's atmosphere and the night caught fire.

The bones of the attack base fell on Terra. Flaring molten red from their descent through the atmosphere, they hammered the continental expanse of the Imperial Palace. Where there was night, titanic explosions created day. Where there was day, millions of tonnes of ash and dust blanketed the sky and brought down a reign of night. Sectors the size of hive cities vaporised. Millions looked up in the final seconds of their lives, and saw the mountains of iron and stone come for them. Millions upon millions more knew nothing. They moved through their entombed lives, far from any view of the sky, ignorant until the blow, the fire, the cathedrals turned to ash, the towers' crushing fall.

Shockwaves annihilated ramparts. Winds of hundreds of kilometres an hour raged outward from the craters.

Firestorms were a hundred kilometres wide. The dead at impact were fortunate in their ignorance or their momentary horror before oblivion. The victims of flame and wind and burial knew terror. Death came to them with great fear and pain.

Victory was choking, burning, suffocating, dying.

Victory was the most terrible destruction for a thousand years.

The greater meteor swarm spared the precincts of the Inner Palace. Small fragments fell closer, pulverising roofs. They slashed the night with streaks of fire. One struck the Widdershins Tower a glancing blow, shattering the plex-glass windows of the Cerebrium.

The big strikes fell beyond Mesring's view of the horizon. The huge fragments vanished, and then he saw the awful sunrises of fireballs. The glow of devastation was the hammer blows of a wrathful god. Then the wind and the dust came for him, reaching into the Cerebrium with a furnace blast. He screamed, then. The hand of the Beast itself had come to claim him. He fell to the chamber floor, abandoned to a monstrous transcendence.

He was not found for two days. Even then, he was still screaming.

FIVE

The Immitis System

They reached the Immitis System, and it was burning.

The Fists Exemplar translated out of the warp shortly after the Iron Warriors. The *Palimodes* was already in combat. A single ork ship was attacking the base in the system. It was a leviathan, much larger than the Iron Warriors strike cruiser, larger even than the Fists Exemplar battle-barges. It was a hulking shape, wider than the *Dantalion* and *Guilliman* combined. A black, snarling, metal beast of war, a thing of shields like tectonic plates and volcanic weaponry, it orbited the industrial moon of the system's gas giant. The ork ship battered the surface with a barrage of torpedoes. Ranks of immense cannons jutted out beneath its hull, running the entire length of the ship. They fired shells the size of Thunderhawks.

At this distance, the moon appeared in the *Dantalion*'s oculus as a metallic tangle. It was only a few hundred kilometres in diameter. Industrial works covered the entire surface. The gravity was too weak to sustain an atmosphere, and the belching of thousands of chimneys floated off into the void. The grey mass of twisting pipelines and manufactoria was lit now by blossoming fire.

'Shipmaster Marcarian,' Zerberyn said from the bridge pulpit, 'set course for the starboard flank of the enemy.' The *Palimodes* had engaged the port. 'Weapons masters, target shields and weapons.'

Marcarian looked up from the throne. 'Not the engines?'

'No. The vessel's orbit is too close to the moon. Anything like a plasma detonation might destroy... our goal.' His hesitation was brief, and he hoped it was not noticed. He had been uncertain how to refer to the moon. It was a world of slave manufactoria controlled by the Iron Warriors. He had just ordered the preservation of a Traitor possession.

Of course you have, he thought. We need the resources to make repairs. I am honour-bound to aid Kalkator for the moment. And I do not intend to destroy a second world on this mission.

The reasons were good. The reasons were true.

They also sat uneasily in his heart.

Marcarian communicated Zerberyn's orders to the rest of the flotilla, and the Fists Exemplar vessels adjusted their course. The ork battleship had not reacted to their presence yet. They had the luxury of planning an attack.

'Master of the Vox,' Zerberyn said. 'Hail the *Palimodes*. Command channel.'

'So ordered.'

'Your arrival is welcome, if tardy,' Kalkator said a moment later.

The Iron Warrior's grim humour made Zerberyn's neck muscles tense. It seemed to carry a presumption of brotherhood, one that Zerberyn was unable to reject as fully as he knew he should. He responded as if Kalkator had said nothing. 'You cannot risk the destruction of the enemy.'

'We cannot,' Kalkator agreed. 'Not in its current position.' The effect of the warsmith's voice was diminished by the distortions of the vox. Even so, it was harsh, the sound of spikes against a millstone.

'You plan to board it?'

'We do. We will be in position to attack the bridge shortly.'

'If your ship survives long enough.'

'Quite.'

The orks were hitting the void shields of the *Palimodes* with punishing broadsides. The strike cruiser was surrounded by a desperate flaring of red. Like the *Dantalion*, the damage it had already sustained was considerable. It would not be able to take much more.

'We will launch boarding torpedoes to aft starboard to coordinate with your attack,' Zerberyn said. 'We will work our way forward and silence their guns.'

'Then we shall meet on the bridge,' said Kalkator, and signed off.

Zerberyn became aware of a presence to his right. 'What is it, Brother Mandek?' he said.

'We are fighting alongside the Traitors again?'

'Yes,' Zerberyn said. He was unable to keep all the irritation from his voice. 'Why are you asking? We travelled with them to Immitis. Or did you think we were following them in order to lay an ambush?'

Mandek gazed at him levelly. Zerberyn had been given command of the mission by Thane, but Zerberyn and Mandek had held the same rank until a few days before that. Mandek appeared to want Zerberyn to remember this. 'I needed to hear it said,' he said.

'Why?'

Mandek frowned. Instead of answering directly, he said, 'I've just come from the astropathic choir.'

'Why?' Zerberyn said again.

'I wanted to know if there had been any message sent to the Chapter Master.'

And again, Zerberyn said, 'Why?'

'You have not communicated with him since we began travelling this path with the Traitors, have you?'

Was Mandek refusing to name the Iron Warriors, Zerberyn wondered, or was he simply choosing to state what they were until Zerberyn acknowledged that truth?

This was not the time, he thought. There was a slippery tightness in his chest.

'What is your point?' Zerberyn said. He gestured at the oculus. 'We are entering battle.'

'There has been another message from Chapter Master Thane,' said Mandek.

'Oh?'

'We are ordered to return to Terra with all haste.'

'So we shall.'

Mandek blinked.

'Do think the flotilla can travel that distance through the warp and arrive intact?'

'No,' Mandek admitted.

'Then we will make repairs first. Or are you suggesting we ignore the ork battleship before us?'

The dark look Mandek gave the oculus suggested he wished the Iron Warriors and the orks the pleasure of each other's company.

'We cannot go far in our present condition,' Zerberyn insisted.

These are all true things, he thought. All of them.

'Is there a message for the Chapter Master?' Mandek asked.

'Yes. That we have heard, and proceed as ordered.'

'You will inform the astropathic choir of this message?'

Zerberyn forced himself not to bristle. 'No,' he said. He met and held Mandek's gaze. 'You will.'

Mandek nodded, satisfied. 'So ordered.'

They were both pretending now that the decision had been entirely Zerberyn's.

'Good. Let's kill some orks first.'

The boarding torpedoes from the Fists Exemplar flotilla drilled through dozens of metres of shield. They burrowed through the skin of the ork vessel like worms through earth.

Outside the hull, the vessels of the Fists Exemplar and the Iron Warriors had the battleship surrounded. The strike cruisers *Paragon*, *Implicit* and *Courageous* were so heavily damaged they had to keep further back and within the shelter of *Dantalion* and *Guilliman*, but they too pounded the enemy with cannon fire. The orks had no need for void shields. The vessel's plating was so thick, so dense, that shells burst against it with little effect. It retaliated,

redirecting some of its firepower from the bombardment of the moon to target the ships.

Zerberyn felt the blasts of the gargantuan cannons as his boarding torpedo ground its way forward. He was in the flesh of the enemy, and it shook with each concussion of its immense turrets. 'Shipmaster,' he voxed, 'all torpedoes are breaching the target. What is your status?'

'Our shields are at the limit,' said Marcarian. 'The hits are counting.'

'Get some distance. I want something to return to when we are done here.'

'So ordered.'

The torpedoes burst through the outer hull. They came out in emptiness. Zerberyn and his squad were suddenly weightless as the torpedo dropped. It struck hard, and its front hatch blew open. Zerberyn lunged forward, bolter held out before him.

The torpedoes had arrived in the lower third of a gallery that stretched for over a kilometre towards the bow of the vessel. Multiple levels of catwalks ran along the bulkheads. They led to the entrances to the turrets. The centre of the hull was a criss-crossing of metal platforms, bridges and ladders. In the vastness of the space, the web looked gossamer-thin. Orks swarmed over the structure like insects, running transport trains of shells to the guns, carrying materiel and tools as the web crumbled and shook with every blast of the guns.

They had taken the orks by surprise. Enemy fire was sporadic. The greenskins raged, hurling blades. They overturned their transports, derailing them and sending them and their contents hurtling down on the invaders.

'Destroy it!' Zerberyn ordered. He dodged a rain of gears heavy enough to crush a mortal. 'Tear this structure down!' He threw krak grenades at the base of the nearest scaffolding. Up close, the strength of the construction was clear. The girders were all at least a quarter of a metre thick. It was the obscene power of the cannons and their recoil that subjected them to such inconceivable stress. Ahead and behind Zerberyn, his brothers used more krak grenades and melta bombs.

The explosives went off within seconds of each other. A score of detonations turned the anchor points along a long section of the starboard base to liquid. The blasts melted through the bases of four supports rising from the bottom deck, and their collapse triggered a chain reaction. The tangle of metal web fell. Cables snapped and catwalks whipped away from bulkheads. Orks were crushed beneath thousands of tonnes of falling iron. The interior of the battleship echoed and rang with the avalanche of metal and the howls of the dying. The flow of ammunition for the entire section ended. The guns would soon fall silent.

Zerberyn led the charge towards the bow. The Fists Exemplar alternated between firing into the gunnery compartments in the starboard bulkhead and triggering further collapses of the scaffold. They had left the boarding torpedoes hundreds of metres behind before the orks mounted a true counter-attack.

They came from the upper cannon emplacements to starboard, and from all levels to port, pouring out of hatches and tunnels. The furious green tide flooded the gallery.

'Keep advancing!' Zerberyn ordered. 'We'll kill the guns, then finish off the crew.'

Squad formation tightened. The Fists Exemplar became their name. They were a fist of ceramite, a fist over a hundred battle-brothers strong, a fist that punched through the enemy, leaving blood and flame in its wake. The density of bolter fire was ferocious. On the flanks, flamers washed jets of ignited promethium over the greenskins. Zerberyn inhaled the smell of burning xenos flesh even through his rebreather. The pungent stench crumbled beneath the purging burn of fuel.

The orks shot and slashed at the formation. Their own crowd worked against them. They cut each other down with their own guns. They could not bring their mass to bear unless they isolated battle-brothers. The fist kept advancing, killing orks with every step. It was a long, slow, inexorable blow. The greenskins threw themselves against the formation and died.

'They are doing our work for us!' Mandek voxed.

He sounded energised by the combat. Zerberyn glanced back. Mandek was close to his position, flamer reducing the enemy to ash. He fought with exuberance, and that was the battle-brother Zerberyn knew – the firebrand on the battlefield, not the worried soul he had seen on the bridge of the *Dantalion*.

'Then we should make them work harder yet,' Zerberyn said.

The leading edge of the fist formation threw more krak grenades ahead. They melted flesh as well as iron, and the collapse of the scaffold web spread.

Ten metres from the end of the gallery, after the last of the cannon enclaves, there was a large door in the starboard bulkhead. Zerberyn had just passed it when it blew open. Three monstrous orks stormed out. As big as Dreadnoughts, they were clad in armour that mirrored that of their vessel. They were huge, massively shielded. Two of them wielded what appeared to be power chainfists and claws large enough to peel open the hull of a Land Raider. They flanked the third, who had a flamer nozzle on either arm. It bellowed in eager rage and bathed the Fists Exemplar in fire.

The assault was a flaming deluge that swept over the formation. The temperature inside Zerberyn's armour rocketed and fire covered his helmet. He could see nothing except the burning red. He fired towards the position of the orks, shooting blind, as did all his brothers for many rows of the formation.

'Rush them!' Zerberyn ordered. The flamer would be useless to the ork at point-blank range.

He ran to his right, still firing, still blinded by the unending stream of liquid flame. He could hear the roars of the giant orks over the din of battle, and that was enough of a guide. He pulled out his chainsword, revved its engine and thrust the whirring blade forward.

He collided with a moving wall. The impact stopped both him and the wall. The wall growled. It hit him from the side with something massive. He flew back and to his right, landing in a heap of fallen iron, outside the wash of the flamer, and he could see again.

The ork's flamers launched the promethium with a pressure as high as the volume was enormous. It enveloped most of the Fists Exemplar's formation. The fist had changed direction, had lost some of its coherence, and the flanking

orks were smashing into it with their massive power limbs. The flamer ork turned off its weapon as the flaming mass it had created closed in to grapple with it. The greenskin attacked with piston-driven arms. It hands were strong enough on their own to rip a man in half.

Zerberyn was at the edge of the formation. Smaller orks surrounded him. He kept his back to the wreckage and climbed a few steps, gaining elevation. He severed arms and heads with his chainsword, holding back the tide while he looked for the opportunity to take down the giants.

He climbed another step. An ork leapt for him, arms outstretched to pull him back down into the greenskin cauldron. Zerberyn slammed the hilt of his chainsword onto the ork's skull. He shoved its head down with such force that the beast impaled its throat on a spur of shattered girder. The ork twitched and writhed, helplessly pinned. Its blood poured down the jutting metal angles.

The flames were dying down, and the Fists Exemplar could see again. Bolter shells blasted away chunks of ork armour, but the giants had not slowed at all. Dead battle-brothers, bodies crushed and dismembered, lay at their feet. The flamer ork lunged down and seized a Space Marine. It lifted him clear of the formation.

It held Mandek. His left arm was pinned by the ork's grip but his right was free, and he thrust his chainsword through the ork's jaws. The beast uttered a choking shriek, tightening its grip convulsively. The sword cut through its throat. Mandek strained and hauled the blade to his right. The upper half of the ork's head slid to the ground.

The body twisted to Mandek's left as it began to fall.

Zerberyn had a clear shot at the fuel tanks on its back. He sent a full burst of shells into their centre. His brothers nearest the ork stepped back as the tanks exploded. The blast stunned the other two orks. The flash was dazzling, but Zerberyn's auto-lenses flickered over his eyes, blocking the glare. Now he and his brothers had a few seconds of advantage where they could see and the greenskins could not.

A huge gout of flame erupted over one of the giants. The inferno flowed through every chink in its armour. The ork became a screaming, towering torch, flailing its arms, as blind as its foe had been moments before. The Fists Exemplar surged forward again, pressing their advantage.

The monster began to go down under the concerted assault.

The body of the flamer ork was still standing, like a monstrous idol that refused to topple. And it still held Mandek in its death grip.

Zerberyn leapt off the rubble. He smashed and cut his way through the stunned enemy, rejoining the formation. He skirted the edge of the fist, wielding his chainsword like a scythe, parting muscle and tendons. Orks fell before him, but he was wading in a muck of grasping limbs and blades. Too slow, too slow, he thought.

The seconds fell away, sluggish and fatal.

Mandek was cutting through the dead ork's armoured limb. His chainblade sent out showers of sparks.

Too slow, too slow.

Behind Mandek, the third monster reached out with a claw. It hammered its power fist on the deck. Battle-brothers threw themselves out of its path. The blow was so powerful the deck rippled like water. Zerberyn stumbled as the surface beneath his boots dropped and jerked.

He reached the flames of the burning ork, and he could move faster. He slipped under the arms of the dead ork. He looked up into the leering face of the remaining giant.

A straight shot. Up through the jaw guard of its helm and into its eyes.

He brought up his bolter.

Too slow. Too slow.

The ork's power claw closed around Mandek's head.

Zerberyn fired.

The claw snapped shut.

The ork's face disappeared. Its skull disintegrated. The hail of shells knocked the remains back in its helm with explosive force. This greenskin did not remain standing after it was dead. It fell backward. The closed power claw dropped away from Mandek's headless corpse.

The giants were dead. The number of the other orks was dwindling.

Then Kalkator's voice was on the vox, that double voice of ancient warrior and of something else even older, that voice of an enemy, yet that voice strangely welcome. 'We have taken the bridge, Zerberyn,' he said. 'What is your status?'

'The starboard guns are silenced, or soon will be,' Zerberyn said. He took up his position at the head of the formation once more. The Fists Exemplar moved forward, grinding the orks into the deck. 'The ammunition flow is disrupted. We will be moving to the port side now.'

'We will join you there. The ship will soon be ours.'

'Good.' Zerberyn blinked the channel closed.

He looked forward to his left and to his right as he advanced, shoulder to shoulder with his brothers through the smouldering wreckage of the gallery. They were leaving brothers behind. At the rear of the formation, Apothecary Reoch would be retrieving the progenoid glands of the fallen, preserving their genetic legacy and the continuity of the Fists Exemplar. The brothers had not fallen into oblivion, and they had not fallen in vain. Their deaths gave him sorrow. He found acceptance in the thought of their gift to the future.

It was Mandek's death that bothered him. Zerberyn had been unable to save him. There was nothing more he could have done. He knew this to be true.

And yet...

I did everything possible. No one could have saved him.

He repeated these truths to himself as if they were weak, and must be reinforced or else they would fracture and turn into lies. He repeated them in the hope they would bury his awareness of the other thing he was feeling.

Relief.

Mandek's oblique accusations were silenced now. So were the questions he had asked.

And the astropathic message to Thane would not be sent.

He could not be saved, Zerberyn thought. Snarling, he blasted a charging ork's torso to shreds.

He could not be saved.

He could not be saved.

Every step of the march through the gallery, Zerberyn repeated the words. They began as a refrain. Gradually, they became something more. Something very like a prayer.

He could not be saved.

He could not be saved.

There could be no salvation.

SIX

Terra – the Imperial Palace

On Daylight Wall, Koorland watched and listened to the night. He had hoped to return to find the silence banished. Instead it was waiting for him, between the sounds of celebration, coiling around the lights in the dark.

This is the victory I have brought you, Koorland thought. Perhaps the citizens of Terra did not feel the silence. Or perhaps they were trying to banish it. Koorland could make no such pretence.

The silence of the dead regarded him from the depths of the night.

There were fires burning out there, but they were the bonfires of celebration and thanksgiving. The flames of destruction caused by the moonfall had been extinguished. Most of them. Towards the equator, one of the firestorms still burned. And the devastation would take centuries to repair.

In orbit above Terra, there was more damage. The void war had ended with the destruction of the moon. Many

Imperial Navy vessels had been destroyed. Others barely limped back to port. At least the ork interceptors had been obliterated by the shockwave of the moon's explosion.

Earlier in the day, in the Great Chamber, Koorland had listened to Tobris Ekharth read the tally of victory. Hundreds of millions dead. Entire regions of the Imperial Palace had vanished. Some of the craters were ten kilometres wide. So much dust had been thrown into an atmosphere already dark with pollutants, day had been banished for years to come. Terra cycled through the heavy gloom of evening to the most profound night. Ash fell across the globe, white and grey and black, an accumulation of dry, gritty snow.

When Ekharth had finished, Koorland looked at Kubik. 'Why did this happen?'

'The analysis of this event is ongoing,' the Fabricator General said. 'We may be years from a definitive answer.'

'Then give us a theory.'

Servos hummed. Kubik inclined his head. 'Our adaptation of ork technology is still imperfect. We postulate that we failed to account sufficiently for the variance between our modifications and the originals. It is possible the teleportation of the moon would have been successful had the devices been powered entirely by our own energy sources. The attempted integration, however, failed.'

'The xenos and the human cannot coexist,' Veritus said quietly.

'Well observed, inquisitor,' said Kubik. 'We might hypothesise a technological conflict. One that was resolved with the teleportation of only one half of the moon.'

'To where?' Koorland asked.

'We do not know.' Kubik waved his mechanical fingers. 'The destination is unimportant. Given the energy released, we may presume that what vanished met the same fate upon arrival as that which remained.' The fingers coiled into tight spirals. The gesture looked very like frustration. 'These reasons for failure remain conjectural. We will need considerably more experimental data to obtain a more complete understanding of where we succeeded and where we failed. It is unfortunate that none of our sensors survived.' His optics turned to Koorland. The gaze felt accusatory.

'The equipment on the *Herald of Night* was destroyed?' Lansung asked.

'Scanning and recording devices were,' said Koorland. 'All circuits were melted when the kill-teams were teleported back to the ship.'

'Very unfortunate,' Kubik said. 'Very unfortunate.'

Koorland had felt little sympathy for Kubik's disappointment at that moment. He felt even less now. The crowd noises that reached his ears were the voices of people who had experienced true loss, not the private disappointment of the Mechanicus.

Yet the citizens of Terra were celebrating. Ceremonies were being held in every chapel and cathedral. The dead were mourned, and the Emperor was thanked. The ceremonies began in the false day and continued into the hard night. With the coming of night, the festivals began too. In the courtyards of hab complexes, on roofs of manufactoria, in the streets and in the marketplaces, the crowds gathered. They sang their praise of the Emperor. They celebrated the valour of the warriors who had destroyed the face in the

sky, the face that had mocked them, threatened them, and shouted '*I AM SLAUGHTER!*' at the world for so many days. They celebrated the fall of the face of the Beast. They celebrated as if the war had been won.

Koorland did not begrudge the people their celebration. That they could rejoice at all was cause for hope. But there was a sound he did not like. He had heard it since he had landed, after the Thunderhawks had escaped the meteor storm. He heard it now: two syllables that rose between the prayers to the Emperor. He heard his name.

He was the hero of Terra. He had returned bloodied from Ullanor, only to wreak vengeance on the Beast and banish it from the skies. He was the author of this victory.

Koorland accepted he was the author of this night. He wondered whether it was proper to call it a victory. A battle had been won, at the cost of a new catastrophe. And the war was not won. He had only destroyed one of the Beast's masks. The true monster was still on Ullanor, enthroned in the capital of his newborn empire.

'Congratulations, Lord Guilliman.'

Koorland winced at the use of the title. He glanced to his right. Veritus had joined him at the rampart. Koorland grunted. He didn't ask how Veritus had known he would be here. He did wish it was Vangorich who was standing there. 'For what, inquisitor?' he asked.

'For the Deathwatch. For its official recognition by the High Lords.'

'That was nothing more than what the Council had agreed to, prior to the mission.' Mesring, he was sure, would still have objected. But Mesring had not been present in the

Great Chamber. He was, it was said, *resting*. If so, that was an improvement over raving and screaming. Koorland saw no downside to the Ecclesiarch's collapse.

'In any event,' said Veritus, 'you have what you wanted.'

Koorland refused to rise to the bait. 'If you truly believe that was my intent, you are a fool, and I don't believe you are.'

Veritus nodded once. 'Politics are never your intent, Lord Guilliman.' He emphasised the title, reminding Koorland of what he had become, whether he liked it or not. 'But politics are your effect. You imposed your will on the Council. They accepted the temporary formation of the Deathwatch, and now that it has proven itself, they are forced to accept its permanence.'

'Permanence? You think the other Chapters will consent to its existence beyond the end of the war?'

'And do you think no further crises will arise which would create the need for it?'

This was not a debate Koorland was interested in having. Especially not with the Inquisitorial Representative.

'What I think,' he said, 'is that you did not seek me out to offer congratulations.'

'No.' The old man's gaze was lidded and dark. 'The Deathwatch did well on the attack moon. Your strategy against the Beast is sound. I am curious, then. How will you use it on Ullanor? How will you decapitate the orks?'

Again Koorland wished Veritus away and Vangorich present. He did not trust the inquisitor. Even though he would reveal his plan of attack to the Council, he recoiled from the idea of Veritus having advance knowledge of it.

Koorland shrugged. He had no plan for Veritus to learn. 'I don't know,' he said.

He was surprised to hear Veritus express sympathy. 'I do not envy you the responsibility of this decision. We live in a dark age. The orks are stronger and more advanced than they have ever been, and the Imperium cannot do what once it could. We have fallen far.'

The admission took Koorland aback. It seemed that it was Veritus who wished to speak. Behold a wonder, he thought. The Inquisition seeks to unburden itself.

'I have read the chronicles,' Koorland said, hoping to prompt more from Veritus.

'They are far from complete. So much has been forgotten in a thousand years.' Veritus paused. 'There are archives...' he began, hesitated again, then continued. 'During the Great Crusade, we would have had the means to counter the Beast's weapons.'

'I can well believe it.'

Veritus changed the subject abruptly. 'Have you thought about how the Deathwatch will neutralise the ork witches?'

'What do you mean?' Koorland asked, wondering how much Veritus knew.

'I have seen the Black Templars' data,' the inquisitor said. 'The witches, I would think, are key. Kill them, and you have your decapitation.'

Koorland sighed. Why did he think there was anything he knew that Veritus did not? 'True,' he said.

'How will the Deathwatch destroy them?'

'I don't know,' he said again. Dark laughter welled up from his chest. 'Like you said, if this were the Great Crusade, we would have the means. Vulkan mentioned a special force – anti-psykers called Sisters of Silence – who would have been sent against the witches.'

'The Sisters of Silence,' said Veritus. 'So named for the vow of silence. They were warriors of a particularly rare sort. They were psychic blanks. Their mere presence disrupted a psyker's ability.'

'You seem to know quite a bit about them.'

He wondered how. The archives of the Inquisition were deep, their memories long. But Veritus had the knowledge so easily at hand. Veritus nodded, but offered no explanation.

'Such a force would be a gift from the Emperor,' Koorland said. 'If we could neutralise the greenskin psykers, then decapitation would be possible. But as you say, we have fallen since the days of the Great Crusade.'

Veritus was quiet for a long time. Then he said, 'Not all have fallen.'

'Who hasn't?'

'The Sisters of Silence.'

'*They still exist?*'

Veritus nodded. 'I believe so. Some.'

Where? Koorland tried to say. His tongue refused to obey him. The silence he had confronted since Ullanor rushed towards him, and it was not the thing he had believed. It was not the judgement of the past. It was the presence of fate.

'Where?' he managed, speaking not to Veritus, but to the silence.

'Do you believe him?' Thane asked.

'Do we have a choice?' Koorland replied.

They were in Thane's quarters, in the small office outside his meditation cell. There were the bare necessities for command – a desk, two chairs, a vox-unit. A stained-glass portrait of Dorn covered the lone window.

The warriors of the Last Wall were stationed in the Imperial Fists barracks at the base of Daylight Wall. There were too many empty cells, Koorland thought. Too many reminders of compounded loss. At least some were occupied.

'He hasn't given us much to go on,' said Thane.

'I don't think he has much more.'

Thane shook his head. 'The Inquisitorial Representative is urging you to seek a myth, using a few uncertain clues as a guide. This really was Veritus?'

'And he wishes to accompany you.'

'How reassuring. He...' Thane stopped. 'Me?' he said.

'This won't be the only Deathwatch mission,' said Koorland. 'We can't attack Ullanor yet, but there are other targets that will make a difference. Mine is the ultimate responsibility and command for the whole. I must remain here. So yes, you and Squad Gladius.'

Thane frowned. He drummed his fingers on the desk. 'I will do as you command, of course,' he said.

'But you have another concern.'

'As Chapter Master of the Fists Exemplar, yes.'

'What is it?'

'I have repeatedly ordered the return of the rest of the fleet. Especially after our losses, we need the reinforcement to fulfil our duty of defence of Terra.'

'Spoken like a true son of Dorn,' said Koorland.

'I ask to be nothing else.'

'Repeated orders, you said?'

Thane nodded. 'Most recently just before we departed for the ork base.' He picked up a parchment and presented it to Koorland.

'Is that the response?' Koorland asked as he took it.

'No. It's a message from the Adeptus Astra Telepathica confirming that there has been no response.'

'You have had no news from them?'

'Nothing more recent than what the Black Templars relayed.'

'The worst may have befallen them.'

Thane nodded again.

'That doesn't satisfy you,' said Koorland.

'I have considered that possibility. It could well be the truth. I was cut off from that portion of the fleet, and there were Traitors in the field as well as orks. Even so. All the ships destroyed without being able to send a single message?'

'That does seem unlikely,' Koorland admitted.

'That unlikelihood in those particular circumstances concerns me.'

'With justification,' said Koorland. 'However, what action can you take?'

Thane grimaced in frustration. 'None,' he said.

'You are needed on this mission more than you are on Terra,' Koorland went on. 'And as I told you, Veritus is going too.'

Thane let out a bark of mirthless laughter. 'We aren't just going where an inquisitor points us. We will be led by the Inquisitorial Representative himself. We will trust a High Lord not to take us to destruction?'

'No,' said Koorland. 'We aren't going to trust him at all. He knows the way to where he *thinks* you may find the Sisters of Silence. Use his information. Listen to what he has to say. But the mission is yours. You are a Chapter Master leading Adeptus Astartes. The Deathwatch is not the Inquisition's to command.'

'Agreed. He'll try to assume that authority, though. That's a certainty.'

'His tactics do not appear to be subtle. So far, at least. His power grabs have been accompanied by a clear belief in his entitlement. All the same, be wary, especially when you find the Sisters.'

'You mean *if*, don't you?'

'No.' Koorland spat the word out. If he denied the possibility of failure with enough force, perhaps he could will what the Imperium needed into existence. 'They must be found. Without them...' He stopped himself. Had he been about to say that unless the myths were discovered to exist, the war was hopeless? No. He would not permit himself so unworthy a thought. But oh, the weight of the defeats. It grew and grew, his shoulders straining to hold it up. Even the victories were partial, and came at so great a cost they were difficult to regard as triumphs. And so many victories led only to greater defeats. He and Thane had already found one myth, only to lose Vulkan forever on the blood-soaked ground of another legend.

And now another search. Once again on the sword point of desperation.

'No,' Koorland said again. '*When* you find them. You will.'

'Because I must,' Thane said. His face was lined with

sorrow. He looked over at the stained-glass portrait of Dorn. 'Do you think, when this war has run its course, we will have destroyed all the myths that were left to us?'

'If we do,' Koorland said, 'we will create new ones. If we have to embody them ourselves.'

On the landing pad of the pocket space port, Wienand approached the warriors of Squad Gladius. 'Politics,' she said, 'is a disease.'

The Space Marines were preparing the *Penitent Wrath* to leave from the only launching facility within kilometres of the barracks that had not been devastated by the meteor storm. They would be departing within hours. Veritus had not joined them yet. Wienand had guessed he would not arrive until shortly before the launch.

Thane and the warriors in black looked at her, motionless.

'You have no love for politicians,' Wienand continued. 'Look where the Council has brought us. But politics are inevitable. There is no cure for the plague, and no immunity. Look at yourselves. The Deathwatch is political in its elements, and deeply so in its effect.'

'Why are you here, inquisitor?' Thane asked.

'I'm here to contain the damage of your current infection.'

Warfist growled. 'You think we would accept a second inquisitor on this mission?'

'When that inquisitor is myself, yes.' She walked across the launch pad, stopping near the gunship's ramp. 'I notice you take for granted that I know the nature of your mission.'

'If you're here,' Abathar said, 'then you know.'

'No games,' said Warfist. 'State your intent or leave us.'

'I've already stated my intent. And you are all playing the political game whether you admit it to yourself or not. But you're right, I should be clear. You know Inquisitor Veritus and I do not work hand in glove.'

'You are both inquisitors,' said Forcas.

'Which did not stop him from attempting to have me assassinated. He *did* succeed in having me deposed as Inquisitorial Representative.'

'And?' said Thane.

'You should think of me as a check against his game.'

There was silence as the Space Marines exchanged glances. She waited in their midst. She did not withdraw to give them privacy. They would have to grow used to her presence. She watched them think through what she proposed. She had no authority here. She could only be invited. But if Thane, as mission commander, requested her presence, Veritus would not be able to overrule him.

'Why do you wish to come?' Straton asked.

Because there is great potential in what the Deathwatch is and does, she thought. Because I won't let Veritus seize that potential for himself. What she said was, 'Because I need to see what you will find.' That, too, was the truth.

Vangorich had told her what Koorland planned. 'The Sisters of Silence,' she had said. She had never expected to speak those words. Years before, in the vaults of the Inquisition's fortress, she had read about them, and many other organisations that might or might not have existed in the far reaches of time. She had never believed the order still endured. There was no reason to do so. The Sisters had vanished into a myth-shrouded past. What they represented...

She had not yet allowed herself to articulate what they meant, because the hope of their reality still felt like a forbidden one. Yet when she had spoken to Rendenstein about what Vangorich had told her, and what she planned, she had seen in her bodyguard's face the same need, the same desire to hope, and the same caution. Rendenstein understood.

Thane was wearing his helmet. Wienand could not see his expression. But in the slight cocking of his head, she thought there was understanding.

'You found one legend,' she told him. 'I need to be there when you find another.'

A low, weary chuckle emerged from the helm's vox-grille. 'Is that all?'

She grinned. 'What do you think?'

SEVEN

Sacratus

The Sacratus System was a dark one. It was in an isolated sector in the eastern region of the Segmentum Pacificus, far from trade routes. It lacked any strategic value. The sun that shone on Sacratus was so distant, the light that reached the shrine world was frozen. It was the glint of ice, and the memory of solitude. The sluggish winds of the planet's thin atmosphere stirred nitrogen snows over the roofs of mausoleums as large as manufactoria. The architecture reminded Thane more of an encrustation than of solemn remembrance. Sepulchres and vaults and chapels were built into and atop one another, tumours of granite and marble connected by tendrils of staircases.

Squad Gladius and Wienand followed Veritus down the staircases. The route was labyrinthine and patchwork, flights descending for hundreds of metres or less than five. Sometimes Veritus chose a direction that climbed back upwards for a few minutes, then he would take a sudden turn downwards again. Sometimes he would pause and consult his data-slate. For the most part he walked without hesitation.

'He is sure of his way,' Straton said.

'Very,' Thane agreed. 'What do you know of this world?' he asked Wienand.

She walked just ahead of the squad, a few steps behind Veritus.

'Nothing,' she said. 'I had never heard of it before now.'

'You have not been looking at the correct records,' Veritus said without looking back. The old man took the stairs with a surprisingly limber gait, even in his environmental suit.

'Oh? And which ones were those?'

Veritus didn't answer.

Eventually the staircases were no longer in the open air. The Deathwatch moved past and through shrines that had been buried by the others.

'This is an underhive of remembrance,' said Forcas.

Thane shone his light over the statuary. 'What era is this from?' he asked Veritus.

'The Great Crusade,' Veritus said, 'and a few centuries after. Then it was forgotten.'

Thane supposed he should not be surprised. Sacratus was off the trade routes. There were no habitable planets in the system and it had no strategic value. He could imagine the memory of the world fading until it was a name on mouldering lists. That did not explain how Veritus knew of its existence.

At last they reached a door guarded by two caryatids in ancient armour. Their mouths were covered by grilles in the form of Imperial eagles.

'You've been here before,' said Wienand.

'No,' Veritus replied.

They passed through the high arch between the caryatids. A domed space lay beyond. Sarcophagi ringed the periphery, and statues lay in repose on each tomb. They wore the same armour as the tomb's guardians. Veritus pointed upward.

'There,' he said. 'That is what we've come to see.'

The Space Marines directed their lamps at the dome. Its fresco, dim with age and frost, depicted a group of female warriors. Cloaks billowed behind their armour, blending together, becoming thunderclouds edged with fire. The women held their swords upraised, converging towards the centre of the dome, where a red sun blazed.

'The stars,' Abathar said.

'Yes,' said Veritus. 'That is what we came here to learn.'

The red sun was at the centre of a pattern of stars, Thane now saw. 'A chart,' he said.

'Of where?' said Wienand.

'Of the location of Vultus,' Veritus said. 'One of the principal fortresses of the Sisters of Silence. This one is close to the edge of Imperial space. If unsanctioned psykers hoped to find refuge at the frontier, they were mistaken.'

'What makes you think we'll find them there?' Thane asked.

'I have accounted for the other, less remote fortresses. They are all abandoned.'

'That doesn't explain why this one won't be,' said Wienand.

Veritus shrugged. 'That is where we must go,' he said.

* * *

The *Herald of Night*'s Navigator identified Vultus' system as Extorris. When the strike cruiser translated from the warp, the red giant filled the oculus with sullen crimson light.

'Hostile contacts!' the Master of the Auspex called out.

'The orks are here?' said Adnachiel.

'Yes, lord.'

Thane stood with the rest of the squad and the two inquisitors around the tacticarium table. He watched the pict-screens light up with the configurations of the enemy deployment. The orks had a small fleet stationed above a moon of the gas giant fourth from the star.

'Two battleships,' Adnachiel said from the pulpit. 'Five cruisers.'

'What are they doing out here?' Wienand wondered.

'Saving us time in our search,' said Adnachiel. 'We know where we are heading now.'

'Lord,' said the auspex officer, 'the vessels are not attacking.'

'What?'

'We are picking up heat emissions suggesting launches, but no bombardment. We are also detecting some launches from the moon's surface.'

'Missiles?'

'No, too slow. I would suggest orks returning to the motherships.'

Adnachiel turned around to face Thane. 'This is your search,' he said. 'Your determination.'

'This doesn't sound like combat,' said Thane.

'It does not,' Adnachiel agreed. 'It sounds like the end of an engagement.'

We can't be too late, Thane told himself. If the orks had won so easily, their search had been pointless from the start.

'We need to see for ourselves,' he said.

'Why are the orks here?' said Abathar. 'The question is significant.'

Thane nodded. 'We need to go in.'

Adnachiel kept the huge orb of the gas giant between the *Herald of Night* and the ork fleet. Shipmaster Aelia brought the strike cruiser as close to the atmosphere as possible, deep within the planet's ferocious magnetosphere. The *Penitent Wrath* launched just over the horizon from the greenskin ships. Qaphsiel, the Thunderhawk's pilot, skimmed the cauldron of the emerald atmosphere until he had a straight shot up to the planetside face of the tidally locked moon.

The satellite was a small one, a craggy barren rock not much more than a hundred kilometres in diameter. Qaphsiel flew low above the surface, twisting through jagged canyons.

'If you have any knowledge of the fortress,' Thane said to Veritus, 'it would be useful to hear it.'

'You know as much as I do,' the inquisitor said. 'My knowledge ended on Sacratus.'

'Then you will remain with the *Penitent Wrath* until we have a secured position.'

'No,' Wienand said. 'We will follow with all due caution, but we're coming with you.'

'Why?' Thane asked. He indulged in some heavy irony. 'Don't you trust us?'

'We need to see,' Wienand said, and Veritus nodded.

Thane disliked the unanimity the inquisitors were showing. Wienand's tone, though, was more urgent. When she said *we*, it sounded like *I*. He thought about trying to force them to stay. He decided against it. If they got themselves killed, he would not mourn the loss.

The surface of the moon became more deeply scarred as the Thunderhawk drew nearer the fortress. The canyons were narrow, deep and interconnected. Soon the *Penitent Wrath* was flying through a landscape as cracked and shattered as glass, as if the gunship were approaching the site of a great blow.

Qaphsiel took the Thunderhawk up out of one gorge, then immediately dropped into a crevice no more than fifteen metres wide and hundreds deep. It cut almost directly towards the coordinates where the *Herald of Night*'s long-range auspex scans indicated Vultus stood. Thane felt the webbing of his grav-harness strain as Qaphsiel took hard turns between the rock walls.

A few minutes later, the crevice opened up into a deep, narrow bowl.

Looking through a viewing block, Wienand said, 'This was a world shaped to their purpose.'

'Indeed,' Thane agreed.

Rising from the bowl was an immense column. It towered a hundred metres above the lip of the bowl, and it was over a kilometre wide. Vultus sat like a bird of prey on its peak. The fortress had been carved out of the rock of the column, the dark stone shaped into harsh towers. Their facades were perfectly vertical. Their angles, little eroded after a thousand years, were sharp as blades.

Qaphsiel flew just above the floor of the bowl as he closed in on the column. The orks appeared to have landed in the area beyond the bowl and on the launch pads Thane could see projecting from the column and the base of the fortress. As he watched, a ship lifted off one of the platforms. It trailed a long stream of fire in the thin atmosphere.

'They're leaving,' Wienand said.

'Some of them.' Qaphsiel had gone into a steep climb. The features of Vultus were becoming clearer. So were the shapes of other ork vessels, their wings overhanging the edges of the platforms.

'They can't help but see us soon,' said Veritus.

'If they look,' said Abathar.

'I have a target for insertion,' Qaphsiel said over the gunship's vox. 'The defence batteries directly above us.'

'A good choice,' Straton said. 'There are no landing platforms on this face of the fortress.'

Unless the orks were using the guns. Thane brushed away the pessimistic thought. Whatever the orks wanted with Vultus, he did not believe they had come to seize it and hold it against non-existent enemies.

'Make ready,' Thane said. He detached the grav-harness. He stood. Leaning against the sharp angle of the ascent, he moved to the side door and slid it back. A hot wind raged through the troop compartment. The Deathwatch squad gathered behind him.

The *Penitent Wrath* levelled off as it reached the height of the fortress. A domed building hulking in the centre of the complex gave Thane the impression of a structure closed in on itself. Its nature seemed to float ambiguously between refuge and prison.

There were windows in the towers. They had all been smashed. Wedges of armourglass glinted like teeth in the red light of the sun.

Qaphsiel lowered the Thunderhawk over a gun emplacement halfway up. The platform was wide, and ran most of the length of the facade. Silent cannons waited to destroy any enemy who would dare approach Vultus. The enemy had come, though. The enemy was doing what it willed, and the guns remained silent.

Squad Gladius jumped from the gunship. The *Penitent Wrath* dropped back down the column, and Thane led the way at a swift march to the nearest entrance. The plasteel door had been smashed down from the inside.

The passageway beyond was dark. The fortress had no power. It was inert as dead as the rock of its walls. Aggressive life moved through the tomb, though. Brutes growled in the distance. Things smashed. But there was no gunfire. There was no battle.

'The Sisters of Silence are not here,' Forcas said.

'There would be fighting,' Wienand agreed.

'And I would feel them,' said Forcas. 'I would feel the pressure of the psychical null.'

'This is futile,' said Warfist.

'The cannons we passed have not been serviced for a long time,' Abathar put in. 'It is highly unlikely the orks have defeated the Sisters. Vultus has been abandoned. Perhaps for centuries.'

'Our search ends here, then?' Straton asked.

'Perhaps not,' said Wienand. 'The dome on Sacratus showed us the way here. Maybe this dome has a similar message.'

The chances seemed remote to Thane. But we have to find them, he thought. Any possibility was worth exploring. 'We make for the dome, then,' he said. 'Silent kills. We have not come to fight an entire ork fleet.'

Warfist growled low in his chest, the sound predatory in anticipation. He took point, lightning claws extended. The rest of Squad Gladius drew blades. Wienand took out her laspistol. 'I'll use it only if we are discovered,' she said.

Veritus carried no weapon.

'You are not very formidable, inquisitor,' Warfist said.

'In combat, no,' said Veritus. 'Nor am I a fool.'

Yet here we are, Thane thought.

They moved into the corridor. The walls were bare, the shredded remains of tapestries lying at their base. The first intersection was littered with overturned pedestals and smashed statuary. A severed head, its mouth covered by the same eagle grille as the caryatids of Sacratus, stared at the ceiling, judgement hard as the void in its blank eyes.

The route to the dome was obvious. The passageway from the gun emplacements ended at a corridor wide as an avenue. Traffic would once have moved rapidly from one end of the citadel to the other, down great halls radiating like spokes from the dome. Vehicles had come down this route very recently. The air stank of spent fuel. The walls were marred by wide scorch marks, and for as far as Thane could see in the light cast by their helms, broken statues lay on the floor.

'The vandalism is systematic,' Forcas said. 'There is hatred here.'

'The orks recognise the threat of the Sisters of Silence,' said Veritus.

'How?' Wienand asked. 'Have they encountered them before?'

'These ork witches are powerful,' said Forcas. 'Perhaps, as a collective, they can sense the presence of a threat somewhere. They're searching too. Seeking to destroy the threat, and any trace that it ever existed.'

From far down the corridor came growls and the sounds of smashing stone.

'We will not surprise them on this route,' Warfist said. He turned off the wide hall at the first opportunity, finding a narrow passage running parallel, and loped ahead of the rest of the squad. He had removed his helm, and he paused at intersections to sniff the air.

The further the Deathwatch went, the louder the ork din became. The sounds bounced off the stones of Vultus, redirected by the whims of the architecture.

'Auspex?' said Thane.

'Unhelpful,' Abathar replied. 'The biomass is too large and mobile, and we do not know the floor plans of this fortress. I cannot narrow the enemy's location and movements to specific halls.'

Warfist held up a hand. Helm lights switched off. Thane blinked through to thermal sight. Warfist was motionless.

'Approaching,' the Space Wolf voxed. He prowled forward, a silent giant, then turned left into another branching corridor and vanished.

Thane waited. Sounds grew sharper. Booted feet were coming closer. The snarls were close, not echoes. Metal scraped against stone. Thane's lenses picked up heat silhouettes. Then light reappeared. A large group of orks came down the corridor at a fast march. They shouted at each other as they dragged their blades along the engravings on the walls. The lead ork wielded a jagged cleaver in each hand. The beast was large enough to gouge both walls as it ran.

'Take them,' said Thane.

Forcas struck first. The blow was silent. Its effect was not. The lead ork stumbled. It screamed. It dropped its weapons and clutched its head. It fell to its knees. The mob behind it milled in confusion. The agony of their leader held the greenskins' attention. They did not shine their lights further down the corridor. They did not think to suspect an attack.

The leader's howls became a hissing rasp, pain exceeding the body's ability to express it. Scalding blood erupted from its eyes and ears and mouth. Crimson steam filled the hall. The chieftain's body fell forward at the same moment that Warfist hit the orks from behind. He jabbed out with his lightning claws, stabbing through the necks of two greenskins at once. Thane heard his satisfied grunt on the vox.

Thane and Straton rushed on, Abathar and Forcas following more slowly. The orks heard the pounding of ceramite boots and finally looked up, much too late. Thane and Straton cut into the greenskins with chainswords. The snarl of the blades rattled the stones of the hall, yet it was of a kind with the howls of the orks and the roar of their weapons. The orks' guns were still strapped to their belts. They had

thought they were alone in the fortress. Thane wanted the
delusion preserved for the rest of the force.

'No firearms,' he voxed to the squad.

'Good,' said Warfist.

Thane ran his blade through the chest of one ork. He
yanked it from the falling corpse with such violence that
the edge of the blade plunged into the shoulder of the ork
to his right, severing the arm, then grinding through the
beast's spine. Straton clashed with a greenskin almost as
big as the dead leader. He angled his chainsword and cut
through the head of the ork's hammer, so the xenos weapon
fell into two halves, and the Ultramarine's blade continued
downward, cleaving the monster's skull.

Abathar's plasma cutter burned through eyes and throats,
the hiss of its beam unheard in the tumult. Forcas boiled
the blood of another ork. Warfist killed two more before the
rest of the mob at last realised death had come for them in
both directions. They lashed out, and they were strong in
their rage.

The Deathwatch was precise.

Thane and Straton pressed in hard. There was no room
in the narrow passage for the orks to find their footing and
use their mass. They had no momentum behind their blows.
An axe crashed against Thane's helmet. His ears rang. He
brought his chainsword up through the ork's gut. The huge
body shuddered. There was a second, weaker blow of the
axe before it fell from dead fingers.

Squad Gladius waded deeper into the greenskins. Thane's
senses were submerged in the thick, liquid stench of gout-
ing blood and greenskin musk. Claws and blades and tusks

and straining muscle tried to fell him. He cut the tide back. He and his brothers in black forced it down. Ultramarine doggedness meshed with Space Wolf savagery, with Blood Angel precision and Dark Angel relentlessness. The machine rendered the orks to bloody meat. Thane had seen the fusion of battle philosophies on the attack moon, in the desperation of that struggle. He saw it again now, the interlacing occurring automatically, triggered by the moment of conflict. As the last of the orks fell, he began to understand why the Council felt so threatened by the Deathwatch.

This was a new force for war.

Wienand watched the five Space Marines take apart a score of orks in a matter of seconds. She realised Veritus was looking at her. 'What is it?' she said as the squad moved on. Her boots splashed through a pool of blood.

'That skirmish didn't mean anything,' said Veritus.

'Your point?'

'Any squad of Adeptus Astartes would have made short work of those orks.'

'I see,' she said, as if she accepted what Veritus was saying. Her interest in the Deathwatch threatened him, she thought. Good.

Veritus was right. He was also obfuscating. The importance of what Wienand had watched lay not in the challenge this group of orks had presented, but in the manner the squad had eliminated them. The disparate operated in unison, forming a lethally efficient whole. *That* was what was important.

The Deathwatch encountered two more ork patrols on

the way to the dome. Warfist varied the route, switching corridors every few junctions, sometimes backtracking or travelling laterally for a brief period before returning to the original heading. The orks went down quickly each time, with no shots fired. The rest of the orks in the fortress never had the chance to learn what had come among them.

This deep in the fortress, they were surrounded by the clamour of the orks rampaging through chambers and halls, smashing all they found. The infernal choir of xenos roars was a mixture of triumph, rage and frustration. The orks had come to destroy an enemy that had vanished from these halls centuries before.

The Deathwatch entered the main hall again for the last hundred metres before the entrance to the dome.

'We should wait,' Forcas said. 'There is a battle ahead that it will serve no purpose to engage.'

'Ork witches?' Thane asked.

'Yes,' said Forcas. 'Several.'

'The auspex indicates a large horde,' Abathar said.

Warfist snorted. 'I can hear it, Techmarine.'

The squad withdrew into an alcove. The entrance to the dome glimmered with light from the space beyond. Wienand could make out the movement of hundreds of large bodies. The dome rang with bestial shouts. There were flashes of energy too, which made her skin crawl. The flares were powerful, the colours somehow inherently inhuman. At intervals, the clamour of the mob faded and individual ork voices rose to prominence. The horde was listening. Wienand listened too, to the sound of the greenskin witches. There was no sense to the language, but she could hear the power. She glanced at Forcas. Deep in the shadows of his psychic hood, his eyes glittered. His concentration was ferocious.

These were the voices they must silence, Wienand thought. She felt the tension in the squad as the warriors held back from battle. They understood the necessity of restraint. And they resented that necessity.

'How long must we wait here?' Warfist growled.

'Until they go,' said Thane.

The Space Wolf growled. 'This is shameful.'

'Shame,' said Forcas, 'would come in failing the mission by rushing into a pointless fight we could not win.'

Warfist muttered something Wienand could not make out. Then he was silent again.

It was several hours before the orks tired of the dome. They streamed out of multiple doors. Three armoured transport vehicles thundered past the squad's alcove. Behind them came well over a hundred orks. After they passed, Wienand could hear the fading sounds of other parties heading out in other directions from inside the dome.

Quiet fell at last beyond the doorway. Thane waited another few minutes, then nodded and led the way into the dome. In the distance, Wienand could still hear the orks ransacking Vultus. There was also the deep roar of ships taking off from the landing platforms. The greenskins were not yet done with the fortress, but the departure was accelerating.

She wondered if the orks had found a destination.

The Space Marines played their helm lights over the hall beneath the dome. They fanned out across the vastness.

'What are we looking for?' Straton asked.

'Anything,' said Thane.

'The orks didn't *leave* anything,' Warfist observed.

The floor was a mass of wreckage. Wienand assumed there had been statuary here, but there was nothing left of it now. She had to clamber over mounds of rubble to reach the centre of the hall.

There had been something large there before, but now there was only a massive heap of ruined stone. There were angled chunks of marble and vague shapes suggestive of massiveness. A colossus of the Emperor, perhaps. A figure to tower beneath the dome, to inspire with majesty. Gone now, reduced to nothing, significance turned to dust.

Veritus wandered between the mounds a little distance away. Wienand called to him. 'If we find nothing, then what?'

No answer.

You thought the Sisters of Silence would be here, didn't you? she thought. You don't have an option beyond this.

'There's nothing up there,' Straton said.

Wienand craned her head back. The squad's beams moved over the interior of the dome soaring far above. There was no fresco as there had been on Sacratus. There was nothing at all. Only darkness.

'Did the orks destroy what was there?' Thane asked.

'It would appear not,' Abathar said. 'The stone itself is black. I perceive some smoke damage, but not much else.' A few moments later he said, 'There is evidence of scoring. The dome may have been scraped.'

'By the orks?' said Thane.

'No. The scoring is beneath the smoke. It was done centuries ago.'

'There's no gallery,' said Wienand. The walls of the hall rose uninterrupted to the base of the dome. 'No way for the orks to get up there.'

'And no reason for them to do so,' Warfist said. He sounded disgusted. 'This is futile.'

Wienand was still looking up at the hemisphere of darkness when the beams went away, and so she saw the light that stayed behind.

'Wait,' she said. She stared, wondering if she was hallucinating. There was a silvery glow around the base of the dome. It was so faint, it vanished when Wienand looked directly at it. She focused her gaze instead on the crown. The silver grew stronger in her peripheral vision. She perceived brighter points and the hint of tracery. 'There is something. A faint phosphorescence.'

The Space Marines and Veritus moved towards her position. They turned off their lights. The hall fell into pitch darkness. Wienand could see the glow more clearly now. She could look at it directly, though she saw nothing more than the most fragile gossamer of grey. 'Those are stars,' she said. 'It's another chart.'

'One that someone sought to obliterate,' said Abathar.

'Can you make a record of it?' Thane asked.

'Yes. It is too faint for pict inscription, but I am making a copy of the stars' positions relative to each other.'

'Will that be enough for the Navigator?'

'We will hope it is.'

'I see nothing in the centre,' said Straton. 'Is something

missing? Is it possible all that remains is the edge of the chart?'

'Unlikely,' said Abathar. 'The scoring cuts across the full height of the dome. The phosphorescence is limited to the lower third. There is...' He trailed off.

'What is it?' said Thane.

'I am uncertain. The pattern I have recorded is suggestive, but we will have to wait for confirmation aboard the *Herald of Night.*'

'Suggestive of what?' said Thane. 'I trust your conclusions, Brother Abathar.'

'If this is a chart, it points to nothing at all.'

'You mean there is no direction?' said Veritus. 'Or that it is unreadable?'

'Neither, inquisitor. I mean as I say – nothing. The crown of the dome is between systems. There truly is nothing there.'

EIGHT

The Western Reaches of the Segmentum Pacificus – the void

The *Herald of Night* came to the nothingness and found hordes. Instead of dark, there was the flare of engines, the flash of launches and guns, the streak of missiles. The orks besieged a point where there should have been emptiness.

There was a single planet in the starless night. It was a rocky mass, so cold its atmosphere was frozen, sullen snow. But the orks had brought heat to the world. Their bombardment melted nitrogen and methane. It pounded the surface to a molten orange, as if the greenskins sought to turn the world into a flowing, liquid hell.

But the world resisted. It remained solid. And the target of the orks' hatred struck back.

'Lance fire from the surface,' said Adnachiel. He pointed to a spike of icons on a pict screen, and looked around the tacticarium table at the Deathwatch and the inquisitors. 'You were right,' he said. 'By the Throne, I don't think I can credit it even now. But I congratulate you. We have found our myths.'

'At war,' said Thane. 'The orks have found them too. Before us.'

'They wasted no time,' said Straton.

'No,' said Adnachiel, 'these are not the orks we saw over Vultus. The ships are different. The fleet is larger.' He paused, his eye caught by a change on the pict screen to the left of the table. He grunted. 'Cannon fire from the surface now too. And the orks have just lost an escort vessel. Impressive.'

'But insufficient,' Thane said.

Adnachiel nodded. 'There are heat signatures of landing craft. The greenskins are attacking on the surface as well.' He frowned. 'What I do not understand is, if they already knew the location of the Sisters of Silence, what interest did they have in Vultus?'

'Fear,' said Veritus. 'Or something very like it. The orks sense the threat the Sisters of Silence represent. They seek to destroy all trace of them.' He pointed to the centre of the tacticarium table. The hololithic display of the planet had an illuminated target. Its coordinates marked the focus of the orbital bombardment and the ork landings, and the origin of the surface fire. The *Herald of Night* was as yet too distant for the auspex array to form an image of the fortress itself. But the citadel was there, its existence confirmed by the conflict. 'The orks cannot know that this is the one place in the galaxy where the Sisters of Silence may be found. They must attack every trace of them they find.'

Warfist bared his teeth. 'If this is true, so much the better. The thought of orks feeling threatened cheers me enormously.'

'It proves the importance of our mission,' Thane said. He

examined the relative positions of the strike cruiser and the ork fleet. 'What is your evaluation?' he asked Adnachiel.

'Worse than Vultus. This ork fleet is not much larger, but that one was already large enough. There are no planets to use as cover for our approach. The orks will see us coming, if they have not already detected our presence. If we fight...' He stopped for a moment.

'No one doubts your skill or the strength of your ship,' said Thane.

'I hope no one doubts my intelligence, either,' Adnachiel replied. 'The numbers and the forces are what they are. We can fight. We cannot win.'

'We have not come all this way for a pointless sacrifice,' said Warfist.

Adnachiel gave the Space Wolf a curt nod. 'Quite,' he said.

'Then our attack must be in two stages,' said Thane. 'We must neutralise the fleet before we engage with the orks planetside.'

'Obviously,' said Wienand. 'But what is the plan to do that?'

Thane had no illusions about the situation. He could see many ways for it to end in disaster, and knew there were many more he had not imagined. Even so, his lips pressed into a taut smile. 'I thought it was clear,' he told Wienand. 'We are going to destroy an ork fleet.'

'The *Herald of Night*?'

'No. The Deathwatch.'

Five Space Marines in a single boarding torpedo came for the fleet. The launch of the torpedo, from the limit of its

range, signalled the opening of a new front for the orks, though they did not know it. Abathar steered at an angle away from the *Herald of Night*, putting distance between the torpedo and its source. The Deathwatch streaked through the void, a lone missile directed at a fleet, beneath notice as the greenskins poured their wrath on the world below them.

The target was the largest of the battleships at the centre of the ork formation. Thane watched the readout of the vessel grow on the torpedo's navigation pict screen. The representation began as a single point. It became an outline, then an ever-more detailed schematic in red lines. Icons for possible attack points multiplied.

'Have you chosen?' Thane asked.

'Yes,' said Abathar. His servo-arm pointed at the screen, to the junction of the immense engine block and the rest of the hull. The vessel narrowed slightly there. The battleship's construction was a brutal monumentalism, a welding together of the massive. But still there was a junction. The shielding and the hull would be thinner. And the location was close to the goal.

'Good,' Thane approved. 'And the ship's position?'

'Within an acceptable risk,' Abathar said. 'The defensive fire from the planet is pushing the greenskins back. They are substantially further from the surface than the enemy over Vultus.'

'Far enough, then.'

'Within an acceptable risk,' Abathar said again.

They had no choice, Thane thought. There was no other way of dealing with the ork fleet. What would be an unacceptable risk? he wondered.

Nothing.

The action was necessary. It was the only alternative to assured defeat.

'Time?' he asked.

'One hundred seconds,' Abathar told him.

Thane voxed Adnachiel. 'We are about to make our attack,' he said.

'Very well. We will delay engagement until your signal if possible. The Emperor protects.'

'The Emperor protects.'

Behind Thane, Forcas said, 'We are establishing a precedent.'

Thane turned around. Forcas was looking at the teleport homer on Abathar's back.

'The means we are using,' Forcas went on. 'The tools. The weapons.'

'You think we should not employ them to defeat the orks?'

'The devices are... impure,' Forcas said. He used the word with the conviction of someone who was given to meditating on its meaning and implications. 'Using them has a cost. We have seen that already.'

'They aren't made by xenos hands,' Thane reminded him, though images of the cratered Imperial Palace flashed before his mind's eye. 'They are still productions of the Mechanicus.'

'Their derivation is suspect.'

'Nevertheless,' Straton put in, 'they are authorised.'

'Even under the eyes of the Inquisition,' said Warfist. He appeared to take sour enjoyment from the irony.

Forcas gave a solemn nod, acknowledging the points. 'Yet

the fact remains the technology originates with the green-skins. The taint cannot be expunged through adaptation. We are conscious of its danger. We are using it in extremity. Would any of you wish this technology to have widespread adoption by Imperial forces? By all the Chapters? By the Astra Militarum?'

The others were silent, their faces grim.

'No,' said Thane. Forcas was right. Already they'd had ample reason to distrust the ork-derived technology. Thane imagined the propagation of its use, and realised he was picturing a plague.

'There must be a balance,' Forcas said. 'I acknowledge the necessity that forces our hands today. Yet we must limit the moral harm.'

'Restrict the use of such weapons to the Deathwatch,' said Straton.

We. The Deathwatch. They were speaking as a unified force, Thane realised. And they were discussing situations that extended far beyond the current mission. He had agreed with Koorland that the Deathwatch was a temporary measure. In many ways, it had to be. He knew his involvement was limited. His responsibilities as Chapter Master made it so. Nor could he imagine any of the Space Marines before him adopting the black livery permanently. They, too, would return to their Chapters.

And yet.

We. The Deathwatch.

There was something permanent here.

'Fifty seconds,' Abathar said, recalling Thane to the moment.

The boarding torpedo had no viewing blocks. The pict-screens above the steering controls were Thane's only window onto the battlefield. He watched the columns of icons and coordinates change as Abathar aimed the torpedo at its target. The bombardment was intensifying. There were more and more landing ships descending to the surface. Damage runes were also appearing with greater frequency. The defenders of the starless world were exacting a price from the invaders.

All of the ork fire was directed at the planet. The *Herald of Night* had not been detected.

'The Emperor does protect,' Thane said. 'He does indeed.'

'Brace for impact,' Abathar warned.

Thane stood firm against the coming blow.

The boarding torpedo hit the port side of the engine block's junction. Violent rattling shook the torpedo hull as the drill head ground its way through the immense barrier. There were no void shields, only a monstrous excess of metal between the Deathwatch and their prey. The grinding went on for several minutes. Squad Gladius stood in a line before the hatch door, ready for the moment to storm out of the torpedo. Abathar's head was cocked as if he were listening for nuances in the cries of iron agony.

'We are nearly through,' the Techmarine said.

Thane lifted his bolter.

The torpedo jerked forward, grinding air, then stopped. The hatch blew open. Squad Gladius charged out from below the drill head. The torpedo had broken through into a corridor running fore and aft. The battleship rang with the incessant beat of its bombardment. There was a group of orks to the right, frozen in surprise. Gladius cut them down with a sustained burst of bolter fire and the orks died before they could react.

The corridor was wide and high, yet it felt crowded by the tangle of enormous conduits that made up its ceiling. The walls on either side were an assembly of mismatched and misshapen iron slabs, held together by an exuberance of rivets the size of Thane's fist. Past the bodies of the orks, the passage continued a hundred metres into the engine block before it ended at a blast door.

There were no other orks in sight. 'These seconds are ours,' Thane said. 'Let us make good use of them.'

The Deathwatch moved swiftly down the hall, Abathar in the lead. The Techmarine paused just short of the blast door.

'A Dreadnought could pass through that,' Straton said.

'I choose not to,' Abathar said. He was looking at the conduits above his head. 'A struggle for the enginarium will not serve.'

'Assuming it lies beyond that barrier,' said Thane.

'The presence of a blast door in this location of the hull suggests it does.' Abathar took a step to his right. He pointed at the conduits. 'So do these.' He was under the largest. It was nearly three metres wide. Water dripped from cracks and clumsy welds. 'This one,' he said. His servo-arm reached upward. He used his plasma cutter to slice through the metal in a circle while the rest of the squad trained guns down the corridor. A few seconds later, a large iron disc clattered to the deck. A stream of brown water poured down. A hot wind, foul with a mix of xenos musk and burned fuel, blew from the gap.

'Ventilation,' he said, sounding both satisfied and offended. 'Ventilation and cooling. The greenskins' conception of the machine is obscene.'

'Though powerful,' Forcas said.

'This is so.' To Thane he said, 'This will be my route.'

'Very well. We will keep their attention focused elsewhere.'

Abathar took hold of the edge of the hole with the servo-arm's claw. He pulled himself up until he could grasp the edge with his gauntlets and disappeared into the conduit, heading in the direction of the engine block.

'Now the guns,' Thane said.

There was the long, booming thunder of another volley. The corridor shook. Warfist laughed. 'They will not be difficult to find.'

Abathar moved through the long darkness of the conduit, facing into a burning gale. He tasted the air through his rebreather grille, laden with particles of soot and unrefined promethium. He was conscious of how offensive this machine grotesquerie was to the Omnissiah. He would make the destruction of this ship a worthy offering.

The pipe stretched on and on. The wind grew stronger. He would find his goal at the source of the wind, he was sure of this. It was consistent with the paradox that was ork machines. They were a confounding mix of inconceivably advanced technology and constructs so crude that they should not have functioned at all. This conduit felt like it had been built by creatures who had heard of cooling and ventilation systems, but had no idea of how they actually worked. Yet on his back was a device that was an even more imperfect attempt to mimic technology far beyond the capabilities of the Imperium. The miraculous and the barbaric mixed with no reason, no order.

It would be his privilege to erase it from existence.

As the wind became stronger, so too did a sound that resembled the breathing of a gigantic beast. Close, Abathar thought. He was nearing the core of the ship's enginarium.

After another thirty metres, dim red light worked its way into the conduit. A bit further on, and the conduit became a nexus for dozens of pipes. There were now also many holes in the main conduit. Perhaps they were prepared for other shafts yet to be constructed. Perhaps they were intended to admit air from the chamber beyond. Whatever their purpose, they let in the pulsing, flickering red. Beyond the junction, fans spun. Abathar could see only a portion of one. Its blades must have been thirty metres long.

Abathar crouched beside a circular grille in the floor of the conduit. Below him, in the red glow, incomprehensible machines clustered. They sparked, they smoked, they chittered at each other as if they were alive. Abathar waited. If there were orks about, they had little reason to approach this particular configuration of machinery. He cut the grille free, and dropped through.

He landed in a nest of cables and shadows, a mire of technical perversity. It stretched for dozens of metres in every direction. The only illumination was the crimson, and Abathar turned around until he could see its origin. He was in a chamber large enough to contain the dome of Vultus several times over. In the far distance a massive shape loomed, as huge as myth. In its centre, a grille opened and closed, revealing and concealing the crimson heart of power, a miniature red sun, enslaved and turned into the motive power for the ship.

Many levels of catwalks ran along the walls of the chamber. Precarious spans stretched through the air to connect to the heart of the enginarium and to other, lesser monoliths. Orks swarmed along the catwalks, welding gaps, replacing cables, tending to control consoles bristling with levers that would have needed two mortals to pull. Power flashed at faulty junctions, incinerating orks. Other greenskins were electrocuted by flailing cables. Their shrieks mixed with the braying laughter of their kin, who then moved to complete the lethal maintenance work or die in their turn. Hordes of the dwarfish greenskins hauled the bodies away or dragged bundles of equipment at the command of their hulking masters.

Abathar had landed on the top of one of the secondary power sources. He was fifteen metres up from the floor of the enginarium, and six from the nearest catwalk. Heaps of tangled, metre-thick power cables sheltered him from sight. A few steps to his right, in the direction of the catwalk, was the base of an energy coil, ten metres high, which leaned out over the edge of the generator. The angry red power spiralled along its length.

Yes, he could do what needed to be done here.

Abathar removed the teleport homer from his back. He looked at the device differently than he had in the attack moon. Then he had been carrying untested technology, whose workings and morality were unclear. Now he saw the machine for what it truly was. It was a weapon, one whose use put more than its target at risk.

He had said nothing during the debate on the boarding torpedo. He agreed with Forcas, though. There were weapons that should never be deployed except by the Deathwatch. They must be kept within the confines of that structure, belonging to none of the Chapters, usable only in very specific circumstances. He distrusted the device, yet he would use it now for the Imperium, and in its destruction remove its unclean being from the sight of the Omnissiah.

Abathar moved towards the power coil. He was more exposed here, but the coil would have the energy concentration he required. The plan was not to teleport a moon this time. He did not have to tap into the full strength of the ship's engines. Even so, an enormous level of energy would be unleashed. He stayed low and in the shadows, a machine among machines. There was a serpent's nest of cables attached to the base of the coil. He scanned the radiation with the auspex until he found those that were drawing power from the coil rather than feeding it. His servo-arm claw yanked one after the other from the base.

A warning klaxon sounded a harsh, animalistic braying across the enginarium. Up and down the walls and the deck below, lightning flashed from wounded machines. Overloads and short circuits took more orks by surprise. Greenskins shrieked and burned. Others roared with alarm and raced to regain control of the unravelling systems.

Abathar's actions were having an impact. He was on borrowed time now. The orks were seeking the source of the malfunctions. They would find him soon. He disconnected one more cable, then began the process of linking the teleport homer to the power coil.

He was finishing the first connection when a trio of orks ran down the catwalk towards his platform. They scrambled over the wall of cables and spotted Abathar where he crouched over the homer. They were just out of range of his plasma cutter. He trained his boltgun on them, and shot two into pieces before they could move. The sound of gunfire disappeared in the chaos of the klaxon and the booming beat of the engine. For a moment, Abathar thought he had gained another few seconds for his task.

The third ork jumped from behind the falling bodies, onto a cable heap, then launched itself at Abathar. He fired, catching the greenskin in the shoulder, knocking its flight to the left. The ork went over the side of the generator. Spraying blood, it tumbled end over end. It dropped twenty metres and landed head-first, snapping its neck. But it howled a warning all the way down.

Other orks heard. They saw the fall. They shouted, pointing, and the alarm spread. From across the enginarium, the orks abandoned their stations. The horde closed in on Abathar.

The rest of Squad Gladius followed the seismic pounding of the cannons. There was no time for stealth, and no need for it. Thane wanted the orks to know they were under attack, and he wanted them looking at the wrong threat.

The Deathwatch warriors tore through the halls and up the levels of the battleship at a run. Orks fell before them, leaves in a storm. Gladius struck with such speed that no warning could be issued. The orks were not prepared for battle on their own ship. Their weapons were sheathed.

Their guard was down. They died by the score. The Death-watch left a wake of shattered bodies and decks awash in xenos blood.

The cannons were two levels up from the boarding torpedo. The chamber was cavernous. Colossal guns, their barrels six metres in diameter, moved back and forth in the upper space above the Space Marines' heads, pistoning with each recoil. The blasts rang through Thane's bones. The chamber vibrated, blurring before Thane's eyes with the steady drumbeat of the bombardment. Beneath the monstrous cylinders, gunnery crews worked the controls. The stations were bulky, grotesque complexes, spitting steam and sparks. The air roiled, thick with the stench of struggling bodies, ozone and spent explosive.

Thane, Straton and Warfist charged the nearest crew. Through a gap between Thane and Straton, Forcas unleashed a storm of crimson lightning. The warp energy hit the greenskins and their controls with explosive fury and both burned. Their station blew up, hurling shrapnel and fire across the chamber. Flames licked along cables and ignited pools of fuel. Black, choking smoke spread through the space, cutting visibility. The surviving crew turned on the rushing squad. Warfist reached them first. A greenskin managed a quick burst of its gun, the shells bouncing off the Space Wolf's armour, before Warfist impaled it through the eyes with his lighting claws. Then he was speeding towards the next position.

Thane strafed the remaining orks with bolter fire while Straton climbed the ruin of the controls, up articulated scaffolding. He affixed a melta bomb to the cannon, then dropped down. Thane and Forcas had already moved on, catching up with Warfist.

The Deathwatch used speed against the orks. The surprise of the attack, the explosion of the station and the spreading fire had them off balance. Their retaliation was clumsy. They rushed, and missed.

Speed. Precision. Purpose.

Four Space Marines charged hundreds of orks, and the orks were on the defensive.

Thane and Forcas provided covering fire for Warfist as he closed with the second position. He gutted the orks that blocked his path, and jumped onto the scaffolding. Straton added his bolter fire to the hail, holding down the crew until Warfist had placed his melta bomb.

Then Warfist leapt away from the cannon and joined Straton and Forcas in giving Thane the cover he needed to sabotage the third cannon. Forcas lit up the chamber with more bolts of warp energy, spreading fires and ripping orks apart with eldritch lightning, but now he avoided destroying the controls. Bolter fire, too, no longer hit the stations.

His bomb in place, Thane jumped down from the scaffolding. The rush had stopped. There were more cannons ahead, but the orks had rallied. The crews clustered around the next station, a barrier of rage, and their gunfire had the volume now to be effective.

'Well enough?' Warfist asked.

'Well enough,' said Thane.

The Deathwatch retreated. The Space Marines laid down bursts of bolter fire behind them, but that was the lure. The true weapon was speed. The orks pursued, perceiving

triumph as their enemy fled. The greenskins were fast, but the shells slamming into their bodies slowed their charge. The gun crews wore no armour, and the mass-reactive ammunition shredded their bodies. For the first several seconds of the chase, the orks died faster than they could charge. Then their numbers told, and they advanced on the wings of hate.

As Thane had planned.

The orks reclaimed the gunnery stations on the run. Crews resumed firing while the larger body continued the pursuit.

This too, was as it should be.

Thane brought up the rear, looking back, waiting for the moment. It came when the third cannon, having recoiled after its shot, moved outward once again. The second cannon was crewed once more, and about to roar back to life. 'Now!' Thane yelled. He pulled the trigger on his detonator. A moment later, so did Warfist.

Incandescence lit the chamber. First one, then the other melta bomb detonated, burning through the barrels of the cannons. First one, then the other gun fired just as the integrity of the barrel was destroyed.

First one, then another monstrous shell exploded inside the weapons.

The cannons flew apart. Thunder so huge it had physical force slammed the orks down. Shrapnel like jagged storm shields flew through the chamber. Flame engulfed the space. And now Straton triggered his bomb too. The cataclysm smashed into the weakened first cannon, and the barrel fell. It smashed down behind the Deathwatch, a wall six metres high.

Thane lost sight of the other Space Marines. He ran through fire, the world was fire, and the world disintegrated. The deck whiplashed. He flew through the fire, the world of fire. He landed on collapsing metal. He kept his feet and ran on.

To the rear, the explosions continued. Destruction spread, feeding greedily. Another cannon erupted, and deeper in the hull, a shell was triggered by the impacts of the blasts. It set more off. The battleship groaned as a chain reaction tore apart the interior of its port side.

Thane passed through the entrance of the gun chamber. The flames reached ahead of him, but he could see the rest of the Deathwatch now, and he could see the stairs leading back down the levels, back towards Abathar.

A great thunder resounded. An earthquake shook the battleship, hurling orks from catwalks. One of the connections to the teleport homer broke free. The cable slashed back and forth, spraying lightning. Abathar seized it with the servo-arm claw. He struggled to reattach it and finish the rest of the assembly. The tremors became even more violent, knocking many of the greenskins off their feet, slowing their attack. Some managed to cling to the side of the generator and climb up to his position. Bestial faces came over the edge just as he was closing the last of the circuits. Without releasing his work, he turned the plasma cutter on them.

The power coil wavered back and forth. Metal groaned. The crimson energy flickered, then steadied.

The explosions continued. Abathar had the sense of the battleship suffering wounds at a profound level. Had it been an Imperial ship, its machine-spirit would have been screaming. Abathar grunted with satisfaction. Well done, brothers, he thought. He finished his work, and the homer began to charge. The red glow spread over its cylinders.

Abathar turned from his work in time to put bolt-shells into the skulls of three more orks climbing the generator. On the deck, the greenskins had found their feet. Not all of them were trying to reach him now. The blast doors on all levels of the enginarium were grinding down. Streams of orks flowed through them, rushing to fight the true threat, or so they thought.

'Gladius,' Abathar voxed, 'it is time we departed.'

'On our way,' Thane replied. 'What is our best approach?'

Abathar looked up at the conduit that had brought him here. Though new fissures had appeared in its surface, it still appeared sound. 'The way I came.'

'We won't be alone.'

'Understood.'

He gunned down a group of orks running across the catwalk towards him. Bullets smacked against his armour and dug into the cabling around him. Some greenskins had chosen to shoot from positions atop other generators. He moved closer to the catwalk, drawing their fire away from the power coil and the teleport homer. He had to save ork technology from being damaged by its creators. He stood tall, weathering the hits, placing his return fire carefully, pulping skulls at a distance.

The mercy was that the orks labouring in the enginarium were not the largest or most heavily armed warriors. They were here because they were forced to be by their stronger brothers. Outnumbered scores to one, Abathar held his ground.

The homer charged. The ship's tremors began to diminish. Abathar sensed time running out.

'Gladius,' he began, about to urge haste. He didn't finish. On the deck below, time ran out.

A monster strode through the blast door. It was twice the height of a Dreadnought. Its armour was so thick, it seemed to be wearing the hull of a Land Raider. It carried a gun larger than an autocannon.

'Gladius,' Abathar said again, 'there is no more time.'

'Hold fast,' Thane replied.

Abathar moved to his right, behind the wall of cables once more, further away from the power coil. He braced himself to fight the unstoppable.

The behemoth pulled the trigger. Its gun spat a thudding barrage of solid slugs. They smashed through generator walls and cut through cables. They set off a string of explosions and fires, a line of destruction marking the arc of the monster's aim. The beast brought the gun up towards Abathar's position. It was indiscriminate in its fire. It did not care what it destroyed. It revelled in the mad joy of devastation.

The conduit above Abathar shook with the tread of heavy boots and the concussion of bolter fire.

Abathar aimed his bolt pistol at the ork's skull. He targeted the gap in the armour where the tusked jaw snarled. He fired. The shells smashed the ork's fangs. They punched into the back of its throat.

It barely noticed.

The monster's cannon shells pounded the cable barrier

apart. Massive blows struck Abathar in the chest and threw him backwards. He fell in a tangle of wreckage, his armour cracked, servo-motors slipping and stuttering.

The other four members of Squad Gladius dropped out of the conduit. They fired back into it. The pipe trembled from the weight of the pursuing horde. It began to sag.

Abathar pushed himself to his feet. The giant ork had paused to examine its handiwork. Abathar forced movement into his legs and made for the teleport homer.

'It must be now,' he said.

The Deathwatch gathered around the homer. Orks poured from the conduit. The giant aimed its gun at the power coil. It fired again as Abathar triggered the homer.

And then, there truly was no more time.

NINE

The void – Nadiries

As before, the human and the ork made war in a realm of energy. For an immeasurable moment, the last stop before disaster, the clash of technologies was a stalemate, and the tiniest sliver of the power was channelled in its proper path. The homer responded as it was designed to do, and transferred the Deathwatch from the ork battleship to the *Herald of Night*. Then the stalemate collapsed. The forces of the human and the ork technologies destroyed each other in their rage. Half the vessel's engine block vanished, disassembled past the subatomic. What remained erupted. An event far more traumatic than rupture struck the engine core. A star was cut in half. It died howling.

A shockwave produced by the severing of reality flashed across the ork fleet. The battleship vanished in a supernova cry of light. The wave blasted the nearby ships to fiery dust. Further out, it snapped escorts and cruisers in half. The wave lost force quickly as it travelled and the outer elements of the ork fleet survived. Barely. Ships floated in the void without power. Atmospheres vented through huge rents in the hulls. Fires swept through entire levels, never to be extinguished.

The *Herald of Night* emerged from the deep dark to bring judgement on what remained.

The dislocation seized Thane again. The ripping apart, the disintegration of identity one with the annihilation of reality. The transfer was so much more brutal than with unmodified Imperial teleporters. In the wrench of the process came the sense of a monstrous excess of energy. Of something unleashed. And of a danger to the soul.

The device was bestial. It was unclean.

It was also gone.

Thane blinked, acknowledging his and his squad's return to being on the *Herald of Night*. They shook off the sickness of the translation and made for the bridge. There they joined Adnachiel, Wienand and Veritus in the strategium. They watched the end of the ork fleet through the oculus. Veritus looked grim, disturbed by what he'd seen. Wienand seemed both awed and thoughtful.

'And so it is accomplished,' she said. 'Five Space Marines have destroyed a fleet. Impressive.'

'There is a cost to these actions,' Forcas said. He was breathing heavily. He spoke with a great effort of calm, as if he were still struggling to hold his identity together. His fangs were bared. He kept his gaze on the deck. 'The means we employed... Such things cannot be undertaken lightly.'

'Agreed,' said Wienand. 'Proper safeguards must be put in place.'

Thane glanced at her sharply. She looked back, face carefully neutral.

He chose not to ask her what she meant. The mission was paramount. 'What have we learned about the situation planetside?' he asked Adnachiel.

'Auspex scans have confirmed the coordinates of the fortress. We have bought the defenders a little time.'

'No more than that?'

'The orks landed a large invasion force. The fortress' defences no longer need to be aimed at the fleet, so there is no division of fire. But that will not be enough.'

'I sense you're about to tell me something most unwelcome.'

'We have been picking up a concentrated energy signature. The orks have something very large approaching the fortress.'

'How large?'

'To judge from these readings, a giant walking machine, an ork Titan.'

I was right, Thane thought. That was not welcome at all. 'Can we attempt an orbital bombardment?'

'Not with any assurance of preserving the fortress,' Adnachiel said. 'The orks' intent with their bombardment was purely destructive.'

'While ours is not. Understood. Thank you, Master Adnachiel.'

Thane turned to the others. 'We have a siege to break and a Titan to kill,' he said.

The *Penitent Wrath* descended to the surface of the dark planet. The battlefield was still heated by the ork bombardment, and the temporary atmosphere was an orange-brown haze lit by the explosions of shells and the streaks of energy weapons. Qaphsiel flew as low as he dared over the orks, bringing out the details of the enemy from the great night. The region surrounding the fortress was an obscurity filled with a brutal, shifting mass. The flash of cannons illuminated the greenskins for a fraction of a second. If they knew about the destruction of their fleet, they did not appear to be troubled by it. This was an army on the march to victory.

That victory had not yet come, though, and Thane now saw how the fortress had held out for as long as it had. The keep was built at the top of a solitary peak. The mountain rose from the centre of a crater kilometres wide, as if the molten fountain from an asteroid impact had congealed back to rock in mid-flight. The slopes were steep, almost vertical, and jagged. Towering above the bowl of the crater, the fortress covered the entire peak. It was even more jagged than the mountain. It was a cluster of towers, walls fused together, rising one above the other. At the centre, the tallest spire stabbed at the infinite night. From a distance, it looked thin and sharp as a sword blade. The lower ramparts were studded with automated turrets. They rotated back and forth, cannons raining destruction on the orks below.

The greenskins raged at the base of the mountain. There was no path up. The infantry tried to climb, but was defeated by the cliffs and the punishing fire from above. They retaliated with their artillery. Hundreds of cannons and mortars battered the mountain and the fortress. They resisted. They stood fast. But the constant attack eroded the walls.

It hammered at the mountainside, triggering rockslides. Given enough time, Thane thought, the mountain would be hit until there were handholds up its entire height, or the peak would be shot through and come crashing down into the crater, the fortress falling from the darkness of the sky to the darkness of the ground. Or, the last ork would finally be blasted to dust by the wall guns.

Given enough time.

There would not be enough time. The orks had no patience. They were bringing forth a monster to end time.

The ork Titan was sixty metres tall. It too was a mountain, one of iron. It lumbered across the crater, rocking side to side with each step. Its shape was squat in spite of its height. Thane pictured the walkers the Last Wall had fought on Caldera. This was many times larger. Its head alone was larger than the dome of Vultus. The Titan was fashioned in the shape of a monstrous ork, and Thane could well imagine the machine would inspire the worship of the infantry scurrying like insects at its feet.

An energy cannon emerged from the monster's right eye, turning its mere gaze into a holocaust. There were other turrets all along its shoulders and flanks. But they were not the worst danger. One of its limbs ended in another energy weapon, claw-shaped, an electrode three metres long between the tips. The other arm was a double-barrelled cannon the size of the ones the Deathwatch had destroyed on the battleship. From the centre of its bodily mass another gun protruded, even larger.

The central gun fired. The flash illuminated the entire battlefield. Thane caught a frozen glimpse of thousands of

orks exulting in the roar of their monstrous machine. The shell slammed into the mountainside. The explosion was gigantic. Boulders flew like hail. A dust cloud rose, then fell in the weak atmosphere.

The mountain trembled for long seconds after the impact. The ork Titan took another few steps, then fired again at the same spot. It raised its huge gun arm and let loose two more shots in quick succession.

Thane was sure he saw the mountain weaken. He knew he had not. He could see little of the battlefield beyond flashes, except for those vehicles with lamps. The Titan was well illuminated. It was a thing of brutish glory, and the orks wanted it celebrated.

And yet...

The power of the blasts unleashed by the ork Titan convinced him the fortress was not long for this world.

'Take us above the Titan,' he told Qaphsiel. 'As close as you can.'

'So ordered.'

Qaphsiel flew in from behind. The colossus continued its slow, steady, relentlessly destructive walk. There would be nothing left by the time it reached the mountain. As the *Penitent Wrath* closed in, Abathar said, 'There. By the left-hand shoulder. A platform.'

'Agreed,' said Thane. He turned to the inquisitors. They wore armoured environment suits. 'You are ready?' They were to enter the citadel and speak with the Sisters of Silence. He did not relish the thought of an inquisitor making first contact with the order, but there was no choice. 'Once the Titan is destroyed, we can coordinate the Sisters' exit from the fortress.'

'You are assuming they will agree to do so,' Wienand said.

'I am assuming nothing. But you know as well as I do that the Imperium needs them to agree.'

Wienand nodded.

'They will agree,' Veritus said.

'I envy your certainty,' said Thane. He thought about what it meant to have obliterated the traces of their existence, and to have retreated to a location so absolute in its isolation. He did not think an agreement would be easy to obtain. Qaphsiel had been hailing the fortress since the *Penitent Wrath* had begun its descent. The only hint of an answer had been the appearance of a single point of illumination at the highest point of the citadel.

The Thunderhawk dropped lower. Qaphsiel took it in at a steep dive. Veritus and Wienand were held firmly by their grav-harnesses. Abathar opened the side door and the Deathwatch stood before the opening, ready to jump. There was only a slight wind. The atmosphere was beginning to freeze again. Nitrogen snow blew inside the gunship. A cold beyond words came in with it.

The temperature could not reach Thane through his armour. The readouts of his auto-senses told him what it was. Yet he sensed it, too. The dark and the cold of the nameless world cried out with such force it was as if there were a huge wind, howling loss at the cosmos. This was a place beyond mourning, beyond the grave. Abandonment, rejection, betrayal, judgement, punishment – they were all part of the great night. They were, he thought, the very mortar of the fortress.

The shoulders of the ork Titan were broad and flat, landing

pads, Thane guessed, for aircraft. They were clear except for a single anti-air cannon at the rear of each pad. The barrels were long, stretching across half the length of the shoulders. The *Penitent Wrath* roared towards the left-hand pad. In the last moments of the approach, the orks finally realised there was an airborne enemy in the field. The turrets began to turn. The cannons opened fire immediately, when they were still facing away from the gunship. Their massive shells burst in the air, brief suns in the endless night. Qaphsiel pushed the *Penitent Wrath* harder, racing against the left turret's rotation.

Still behind the Titan, the Thunderhawk dropped below the shoulder, then came back up, flying level. The platform came closer. The turret was a third of the way through its rotation. In another moment, the length of its barrel would be in the gunship's flight path.

Thane braced. He heard the whine of the turbofans as they began to alter the ship's trajectory. Qaphsiel fired the retro-nozzles, slowing the flight. The deck angled up. Thane began his leap with the landing pad still ahead. He was in the air just as the Thunderhawk passed over the edge of the Titan's shoulder. He and the squad landed, rolling off the momentum. The engine whine became a scream. The *Penitent Wrath* climbed sharply, pushing up with all the force of its turbofans. Its nose passed over the cannon. The anti-air guns fired interlocking streams of shells, but the gunship rose faster than the orks could adjust their aim. It flew on, higher, gathering yet more speed as it made for the high spire of the fortress.

Thane rose to his feet. His Deathwatch brothers at his

side, he ran towards the Titan's head. The platform tilted up and down with each rocking step of the weapon. The head was a massive, grimacing icon of a monstrous deity. It was surrounded by a rampart of teeth, the gaps between them like huge, clumsy crenellations. Their construction was as rough, patchwork and monolithic as the rest of the monster. Thane found plenty of handholds. Gladius climbed the teeth and dropped into the space beyond. It was wide as a town square.

In the head's left eye, heavy-calibre guns opened up. Their fire swept across the empty space towards the Deathwatch.

Close in, the fortress was just as angular and bladed as it had appeared from a distance. The towers were clusters of close-standing spikes. They made Wienand think of a forest of lightning claws jutting from mailed fists. Turrets tracked the *Penitent Wrath* as it climbed the heights of the fortress. They tracked, but they did not fire.

'A good sign?' Wienand said to Veritus.

'Not the worst, at least.'

The high tower had a small landing pad just below its tapered peak. It was the site of that single, harsh light. Qaphsiel approached it slowly. A gun mounted into the wall of the spire followed silently. The Thunderhawk came down on the pad. Wienand approached the open side door. The gun, five metres up, was pointed directly at her. She jumped down to the flagstones. Veritus followed her. The gun did not move.

Far below, the monstrous ordnance of the Titan struck the mountainside. The tremors reached all the way up.

At the other end of the platform was an iron door. In the

landing lights of the Thunderhawk, it was a stark black, glinting with methane frost. Wienand walked to the door. There were no handles. She stifled the impulse to knock. They know we're here, she thought. Veritus stood beside her. 'Now what?' she asked. 'Did you have a speech prepared?'

Veritus shook his head. The harsh light mounted on his helmet bleached his features. The shadows of his face were deep as canyons. As he gazed at the door, so utterly closed and cold, he did not resemble the dangerous inquisitor Wienand had struggled against on Terra. He did not look like the zealot who had sent assassins after her. He looked like a very old man, one who had seen too much, who stood at the brink of despair, and who had to fight hard not to fall into its abyss.

No, he did not have a speech.

Wienand wondered again why Veritus had insisted on coming. To observe the Deathwatch? Certainly. There was much to know there. There would be matters to prepare as a consequence. But here, why come to this locked door? He could have just as well waited aboard the *Herald of Night*.

Perhaps he had come to bear witness. So had she. Though she felt another need as she stood here like a supplicant. She did not know what she should call it. She recognised the imperative, though. Even if Thane had not turned this part of the mission over to her, she would still be here.

A minute passed. Then another. Silence deeper than the absence of sound, a silence of the soul, hard and cold, surrounded the tower. At last, Wienand said to Veritus, 'You must go.' When he started to object, she interrupted him. 'You know I'm right. You can't be here.' She looked back at the *Penitent Wrath.* 'That can't remain idle. It needs to be elsewhere. You need to not be here.'

Veritus looked at her. His face was still, unreadable. His eyes were nothing but glinting black. In the end, he nodded and walked back to the gunship.

'Leave me,' Wienand voxed Qaphsiel.

'Understood.'

She faced the door. She didn't look as the gunship took off. Light faded. There was only her helmet lamp now, and the night pressed close. The silence gathered weight. Wienand's awareness of the war faded. There was only the door, and the myth behind it. She could not summon the myth. She could not make the door open. But she could wait. To stand here and meet the tower's silence with her own was the most direct action she had yet taken in this war.

Then the silence changed. There was no noise in the thinning, falling, snowing atmosphere. But the silence changed, because there was movement. Frost cracked. The shadows changed.

The door opened.

From the dark of the Titan's eye, massive stubber fire battered the Space Marines. They fought back with light. Forcas stretched out his arms. Energy flashed from his fingers, golden and pure, a blaze of righteousness in the night. The light became a wall. It was a shimmering nobility. The orks trained their fire onto the barrier. The shells exploded against the golden aura. Forcas strained. The shield trembled, flickered for a moment, then held.

'Get beneath the guns!' Thane yelled. 'They're our way in.'

The Space Marines broke left and right. Forcas stayed where he was, preserving the shield, holding the orks' focus. Thane and Warfist went left around the wall, ran back into the dark. It was lesser, the glow of Forcas' barrier spreading over the entire open area before the Titan's skull. The Space Marines were visible to the gunners, but the barrier was the lure, dazzling them, frustrating them as it resisted their shells. On the other side of the wall, Straton and Abathar had almost reached a point directly underneath the eye turret.

The barrier flickered again, buckling under the sustained fire. In another moment, Forcas would be exposed.

The eye was three metres up the wall of the skull. Abathar fired upward with his plasma cutter. He sliced through the barrel of one of the guns. The weapon exploded. Straton threw a grenade through the socket. There was a second blast. The eye glared red at the night, blazed as ammunition cooked off, then went dark.

At the base of the head, a door in the shape of a maw rose with a deafening metallic screech. Orks boiled out of the opening. Thane and Warfist strafed them with bolter fire and hurled frag grenades into their midst. The charge stumbled into chaos, giving Forcas time to run across the space to join Straton and Abathar.

Thane and Warfist kept moving, and kept shooting. More and more orks were rushing from the maw. They become a flood, and there was no more holding them back.

'We're clear,' Straton voxed.

'Go!' said Thane. He nodded at Warfist, who ran the rest of the distance to the eye. Thane paused long enough to throw two more grenades into the orks and hit them with a wide spray of shells. The orks were lightly armoured. They were the servants of their god-machine, not infantry, and Thane killed many. They were also legion, and their undisciplined shots were counting. Bullets hit him, a cascade of blows, driving him back.

'We're in,' Warfist said.

Thane ran. He'd bought the squad the time it needed. Now the rest of Gladius poured fire on the orks from inside the eye, covering Thane. He maglocked his bolter to his thigh and leapt. Warfist caught his arm and pulled him inside.

The turret was a space of twisted, burned metal and carbonised flesh. The doorway out was blocked. Abathar hauled the wreckage out of the way while the others fired down on the orks as they tried to climb. Forcas created another golden shield over the opening of the eye. The orks screamed, enraged by the desecration of their icon as well as the barrier to their weapons.

Abathar had the way clear. Beyond was a narrow corridor leading deeper into the head. Thane said, 'We have to kill the greenskins that direct this abomination. Can you take us to them?'

'I can speculate about where they might be,' Abathar replied.

'That's all I can ask. Lead us.'

Abathar plunged into the dark, cacophonous shadow. Thane followed. Straton stayed to plant a melta bomb. When the light of Forcas' shield winked out, a more searing brilliance followed. The ceiling of the turret fell in, and the eye was blinded forever. The Deathwatch moved into the Titan, seeking its brain.

The hall at the top of the spire was circular. Vaulted, stained crystalflex windows faced every direction. With no illumination outside the fortress, the windows were lit by their own art. The mosaics depicted warriors destroying the enemies of the Emperor. Many of the foes wore psychic hoods. Their faces were contorted grotesques. Their eyes blazed with the fires of the warp, and the fires died before touching the warriors in armour of gold, of red, of black. Some of the windows depicted vessels, black against the black of the void, distinguishable only because they were outlined by the same phosphorescence that limned the figures of the other mosaics. The interior of the spire was lit the same way. The narrow, pointed dome was yet another star chart.

This one was of the entire Imperium. But the chart was old. It was the Imperium as it once had been, not as it was now. The faint trace Wienand had seen in Vultus was sharp here as a razor to the eye. In the night of the world, the cold silver was stark, nearly blinding, and without forgiveness.

The voice of the woman before Wienand was just as cold, just as lacking in mercy. It was the sound of silver.

'Why have you come to Nadiries?' she said.

Answering was difficult. It was painful to be in the presence of these women. An aura of *nothing*, of suffocating *blankness* squeezed Wienand's soul. She felt as if something had murdered her unconscious mind. She was diminished. If this was her experience, she could not imagine the agony a psyker would suffer in this hall.

What had Wienand expected? Was it this? Was it to see the Sisters of Silence arrayed before her in this solemn amphitheatre?

No.

They wore dark, hooded robes, filigreed in the cold silver. They were wrapped in the void, upon its black the wordless voice of the stars and their memories of endless sacrifice. While Wienand struggled to speak, they pulled back their robes and hoods. The army of silence appeared before her in armour of gold, of red, of black.

Had Wienand expected to face the Sisterhood for the first time like this, standing in the centre of the amphitheatre, facing judgement colder, more pure, than that of the Inquisition?

No.

What *had* she expected? She did not know. But most of all, she had not expected to be alone, to know that it would be her words on which the success or failure of the mission would depend.

She had also not expected the Sisters of Silence to *speak*.

At last she managed, 'We have come to seek your aid.'

'We?'

'The Inquisition, which I represent. The Adeptus Astartes, who are fighting at this moment to save Nadiries.' She paused for a moment. '*We* is every citizen of every human world. The Imperium seeks your aid.'

The woman stared at her. Her armour was crimson. So were the optics that had replaced her eyes. Her face was expressionless, as devoid of light as the world.

Wienand estimated there were fifty Sisters of Silence

present. Some wore helmets. Many did not. Their heads were clean-shaven except for a single long rope of hair. Some bore electoos of the Imperial aquila on their brows. Ritual scars marked their cheeks. Almost all the Sisters wore grilles over the lower halves of their faces. Some had helms with ornate rebreathers that concealed their features entirely. They had new faces of metal. All of the designs connoted a form of silence, though one that found expression in actions so final, they exceeded the power of mere words.

'The Imperium seeks our help,' said the warrior with the crimson stare. She spoke with a flat, deathly tone. 'I am Kavalanera Brassanas, Knight Abyssal of Purgatory Squad, and it has been many centuries since the Imperium made it clear the aid of my order was not desired. I find this request hard to credit.'

'And even more difficult to trust,' said a Sister behind Brassanas. Her armour was black. Her face was one of those entirely concealed. Her voice resonated metallically behind the mask.

'I agree with Knight Obsidian Drevina,' said Brassanas.

'The entire Imperium is besieged by orks,' Wienand said. 'They have technology beyond anything we possess. They have destroyed whole worlds. They smashed the Imperial Fists. The Imperium will fall without your aid.'

No emotion. No answer. Time fell into the dark. There was a faint movement of the Sisters' fingers. They were speaking to each other, Wienand realised. She felt as if she were witnessing the discourse of tombs. They use their cant, she thought, but they speak too. Why?

Brassanas said, 'Perhaps it is time for it to fall.'

Wienand gaped. But the shock made pieces fall into place. The Sisters had turned their backs on the Imperium, as they had turned from silence. 'You renounced your vows,' she said. 'Was it that easy to abandon the Imperium?'

'Our vows were to the Emperor,' Brassanas replied. 'And to the Imperium He created. The corruption you serve is not that Imperium. We still serve the Emperor. We still stand guard against the witch.'

'We do not recognise the simulacrum that has replaced the Emperor's dream,' said Drevina.

'That is the true betrayal,' Brassanas said. 'Let it fall.'

'Let it fall,' Drevina repeated.

'Let it fall,' the other Sisters echoed. 'Let it fall. Let it fall.'

The whispered chorus chilled Wienand because it had the ring of justice. In this hall, there was moral authority of a kind never dreamed of in the Great Chamber. Wienand thought of the High Lords, and saw only the rightness of Brassanas' verdict.

And yet...

In that verdict, Wienand saw the way forward.

'Vulkan would have agreed with you,' she said.

'Vulkan,' said Brassanas.

Wienand sensed a stir in the hall, though no one moved. 'The primarch had no love for the High Lords. He saw the corruption. He knew the High Lords and all their works to be worthy only of contempt. Yet he fought for *this* Imperium.'

'Vulkan was with you?' said Drevina.

'*Fought?*' said Brassanas, emphasising the past tense.

Wienand nodded. 'He died fighting the orks on Ullanor.'

A gasp rippled through the theatre.

'Vulkan is dead,' Drevina said, and her whisper was a mourning cry.

'Vulkan is dead,' the other Sisters repeated. 'Vulkan is dead.' The words tolled. The echoes grieved.

'Ullanor,' Brassanas said, sounding the word slowly. 'The orks have returned to Ullanor. Then perhaps the end has truly come.'

'Perhaps,' said Wienand. 'But Vulkan fought it.'

Brassanas said nothing.

'If the Imperium falls, if Terra falls,' Wienand pursued, 'what of the Golden Throne?'

Still nothing.

'What of your vow to the Emperor? And is this to be your legacy? The destruction of everything the Sisters of Silence have fought so hard to protect? Because you refused to help when you possess the key to defeating the orks?'

'We possess the key?' said Brassanas. 'Explain yourself.'

'The ork witches,' Wienand said. 'Destroy them, and we destroy the Beast.'

Brassanas stared at her for several long moments. Then she said, 'We will deliberate. You will be taken to the lower gates to await our decision.'

'No!' Wienand shouted. There could be no deliberation. There was no choice. There was only duty. 'How long will you deliberate? Until the orks tear down your gates?'

Brassanas watched her.

'I too have been betrayed,' Wienand said. 'I have seen the corruption first-hand. I know exactly what it is I am defending. And I will defend it to my last breath. I will not let the Imperium fall into silence.'

'Sacred or profane,' Drevina said to Brassanas. 'We must choose our silence.'

Brassanas nodded. She threw her cloak back over her shoulders, revealing the power claw on her left arm.

Now there were other echoes in the hall. They were the ratcheting clanks of magazines slammed home, and the impact of boot heels on stone. One by one, the unforgiving saints of the Imperium began their preparations for war.

The ork engineer's gun unleashed a torrent of energy. The coruscating beam struck Thane, surrounded him, and lifted him from the deck. It threw him back between two immense spinning columns. Each was ten metres in diameter, and grooved. They moved back and forth along a horizontal slot in the deck, grinding together, then pulling back. Thane bounced off the pillar to his left, then fell into the ragged tear in the deck. He clung to the edge. Below him, the darkness shrieked with massive, incomprehensible machinery. If he fell, he would be reduced to pulp and splinters of ceramite in moments.

On either side, the spinning pillars closed in. The residual energy from the gun's strike pulsed and jittered through his armour, and it would not obey his muscles' commands. He held on to the ledge, but he couldn't move.

The columns spun nearer.

There were three ork engineers in the control centre of the Titan. Abathar's speculation had proven correct. He had led Squad Gladius upwards through the ork Titan's head, winding through corridors tangled with power conduits and clanging with exposed gears to this point, just above the energy-cannon eye.

A hatch opened in the forehead of the Titan to reveal the land below and the mountain ahead. The space was vast yet crowded, a maze of pistons and chains, of machinery that spread like a cancer, yet somehow moved the Titan forward and directed the aim of its weapons. The engineers laboured in a multi-levelled nest of levers and arcing power sources. Each ork worked at its level, but when Gladius attacked, two of the engineers retaliated with energy weapons. The third clambered up and down the control levels, frantically throwing switches and working the dark machinic sorcery that kept the Titan advancing.

The force field protecting the engineers held back Straton's shells. Warfist raced through the chamber, gutting the greenskins commanded by the engineers and slicing cabling in half. The second engineer hit Abathar with his beam weapon. The Techmarine was seized by a gravity whip, and the ork propelled him out of the hatch. The claw of his servo-arm clamped around a thick cable as he flew, and he hung on. The ork held the trigger down, its weapon glowing with heat. It shook Abathar back and forth, trying to dislodge his grip and send him falling far to the ground below.

A score of orks had rushed Forcas, overwhelming him with sheer mass, pushing him into machinery where he had no leverage. As Thane struggled to pull himself up, he heard a feral roar. Greenskins staggered back. The Blood Angel tore through them with his chainsword and a howling fury Thane had sensed just beneath the surface of his rigid, pious calm. His face was covered in the enemy's blood. He raised a fist surrounded by a halo of scarlet warp energy.

Both ork engineers trained their weapons in his direction. They fired at the same moment he unleashed his incinerating blast. The two forces collided halfway across the chamber. The explosion was blinding.

The Titan tilted violently to one side. The deck slanted. It was enough for Thane to push himself out of the trap. The columns clashed together behind him and the space marine rounded on them, facing a wall of grinding, whirling metal. He threw a melta bomb at the intersection of the pillars and thumbed the detonator at the same moment. The explosive went off before it could be sucked into the vortex. There was another dazzling flash.

Thane stumbled away, regaining control of his limbs. The columns spun into the melting heat of the explosive. They fused with each other, and their huge mass pulled them in the opposite directions of their spin. A huge, shuddering jolt ran through the Titan. From the decks below came the sounds of screams and the vibration of blasts.

The warring lightning faded between Forcas and the orks. The Blood Angel was still standing, but his armour was badly scorched. His face was a mass of burned meat. He staggered forward, still snarling. One of the engineers had fallen, smoke rising from its blackened corpse.

Abathar pulled himself back inside the Titan's head. He charged the engineers' nest and swung his power axe at the straining shield. Warfist looped around and rammed his shoulder into the field at the same moment. Straton's shells never let up. The two remaining greenskin engineers had just enough time to know what was coming and roar a brutish denial.

They were dead moments later.

The molten bedlam of the columns screamed. Its fire spread along the cables. They melted. They convulsed like maddened serpents. Electrical fury lanced through the space and the fused columns spun still faster as they shattered restraints. The whirl reached beyond them. It took the chamber. It seized the Titan. Thane felt a world roar into a vortex.

The ork Titan was going mad.

The entrance behind Thane, the one through which Squad Gladius had entered the control hall, had been destroyed by the maelstrom of the columns. There was another one in the far wall. 'Seal the door!' Thane shouted into the vox. There would be no chance for any ork to attempt to regain control of the Titan.

Straton and Abathar ran through the monstrous clamour of the growing destruction. Abathar melted the door along its seams while Straton placed charges across the ceiling. Thane and Warfist turned to Forcas. The Blood Angel's snarls were inaudible in the thunder of disintegrating metal. His movements were sluggish. They guided him towards the hatch.

The door burst open, the crush of orks overwhelming the seals before Abathar could complete them. He turned plasma cutter and power axe against the horde. He was surrounded by a flood of blood and greenskin muscle.

'Do it now!' Thane heard him vox Straton.

The Ultramarine set off the charges. The blasts brought down shrieking machinery and slabs of metal. They crushed flesh. Abathar disappeared under tonnes of burning wreckage with the horde.

The deck tilted thirty degrees. It threw Forcas, Thane and

Warfist against the outside wall. Straton grabbed a spur of rubble, kept his feet and hauled. Metal shifted. The centre of the rubble glowed white. It trembled, then began to collapse from the heat of the plasma cutter. Abathar reared out of the mass. His left arm hung limp, but he punched at his prison with servo-arm and axe.

The deck rocked back, then to the sides. The rotation grew more violent. The spin gathered momentum. The columns had become a blinding mass of self-destruction, and still they spun and spun and spun. The flames were everywhere. There would be no salvation for the Titan. Soon there would none for the Deathwatch either.

'Qaphsiel,' Thane voxed. 'We need extraction. Make for the crown of the Titan.'

'Understood.'

Warfist went through the hatch first. He hacked at the shielding with his power claws, carving a path up. Forcas sagged against Thane, but he had ceased snarling, and he reached out and grabbed the sides of the hatch. A cloud of fire swept over them. Blinded, Thane felt Forcas begin to pull, and he added his strength to the Blood Angel's, guiding him into the air.

'Straton,' he voxed. 'Abathar.' He looked back, but he could no longer see them. The control chamber was darkness and flame and heaving movement.

'We are here,' Straton answered. 'We are following.'

Thane climbed outside. Fire erupted from the eyes of the Titan. Above him, Warfist was helping Forcas towards the crown. Thane waited until he saw Straton emerge from flame and smoke, then Abathar behind him. Then he climbed.

The mind of the Titan was dying, and its body responded with ever greater violence. The massive cannons were still firing, but the Titan's arms were caught in a pendulum motion, the swings growing longer and more wild. The monster's gait was a drunken, turning sway. It was a mountain falling into a dance of death.

Squad Gladius clung to the skull in storm. The *Penitent Wrath* skimmed the top of the Titan. Qaphsiel flew the gunship in tight circles as the Space Marines reached the peak. Warfist jumped through the side door as the Thunderhawk went by. He reached down for Forcas on the next pass. Thane held the psyker up. He was barely responsive.

'Raise your arms, brother,' Thane said. 'Raise them in triumph.'

Something in Forcas heard. He obeyed. Warfist grasped his forearms and hauled him aboard. Thane and Straton followed when Qaphsiel brought the gunship around again.

One more pass now. One more brother. Thane and Straton crouched at the door to aid Abathar. The Techmarine flexed his knees and began his leap.

Metal buckled. The crown of the Titan collapsed into the vortex. Shields turned to jagged teeth. Abathar fell into the gnashing metal.

He stretched his servo-arm up as he plummeted. Thane seized the claw. The imploding skull dragged Abathar down and sought to pull Thane from the gunship. Straton clasped the arm and they both pulled.

Thane felt the jaws crush something human. The disintegration of bone shook through Abathar's frame and into

Thane's arms. 'We have you, brother!' he yelled in defiance of the dying beast.

Then they did have him. They pulled him free. They dragged him aboard.

His right leg was gone below the thigh.

The Thunderhawk pulled away from the Titan. The monster was out of control now. It staggered through the mass of the ork army, crushing infantry beneath it. Its arms were a monstrous flailing, and the devastation of its guns spread across the battlefield, punching new craters in the ground as well as the mountainside. The ork invasion force turned on its own weapon. The caldera became a battlefield, a cauldron of explosives as the orks struggled against the awful power of their technology gone mad.

The *Penitent Wrath* flew towards the fortress.

Forcas was unconscious. Warfist and Straton wrestled him into a grav-harness. Abathar was awake. His blood slicked the deck, but his Larraman cells had already slowed the flow, coagulation building a scab over the stump. The femoral artery had pinched itself closed. Thane helped the Techmarine to a bench, then turned to Veritus. The inquisitor had been sitting silently in the troop hold. 'Well?' he asked.

Veritus shook his head. 'I don't know.'

'The enemy is distracted,' said Warfist. 'If they're going to break out...' He stopped. 'What is that?' he said.

Thane joined him at the viewing block. The mountain just below the base of the fortress was moving. 'A gate,' he said. A seam of light appeared in the darkness. Walls of rock rumbled apart, revealing a vehicle bay beyond. Silver illumination bathed the cliff face. Three armoured vehicles advanced from the depths of the bay. 'Rhinos,' Thane said.

'How do they expect to reach the ground?' Warfist demanded. 'That's a sheer–' He stopped.

Thane's eyes widened.

'If those are Rhinos,' Warfist said, '*why are they flying?*'

Engine exhausts burned red on the flanks and undersides of the Rhinos. The vehicles streaked down the mountain-side, then levelled off as they approached the ground. The squadron flew over the orks, storm bolters cutting a swath of fire through them. Thane witnessed impossible, awe-inspiring technology, and it was Imperial.

Exulting, he said, 'They are flying because they are transporting myths.'

EPILOGUE

Terra – the Imperial Palace

Koorland listened to the silence. It was stronger than ever. It strode above the celebrations. Its weight gathered second by second, and he knew its cause.

From the base of a staircase wide enough for thousands but forbidden to all but a few, he gazed at the towering door of the Sanctum Imperialis. He would never see what lay beyond. That was perhaps as it should be. The sublime was not for his eyes. He had not earned the right. The women who had entered a short while ago had that right. The staircase was not forbidden to them, nor was this door. There were other entrances to the Sanctum, but they were for those who would never come out again. The warriors who had climbed this staircase would also descend it.

'Did you speak to them?' he asked Thane.

'Very little. They were disinclined to speak to anyone except Inquisitor Wienand.'

'I see.' He pushed aside thoughts for now of the power play Wienand might be preparing.

Inside the Sanctum, fifty women were passing before the Golden Throne, renewing their vows to the Emperor, and swearing themselves to eternal silence. Theirs was the quiet he was hearing. It was not a silence for which he could take credit or blame. It was not his burden, or his sacrifice, or his honour.

He gave thanks for it, though. He did not expect this silence to banish the others. Their weights would remain with him. But it might bring about yet another. Through it, the Beast would at last cease to roar.

The Beast Arises continues in Book 10

The Last Son of Dorn
by David Guymer

September 2016

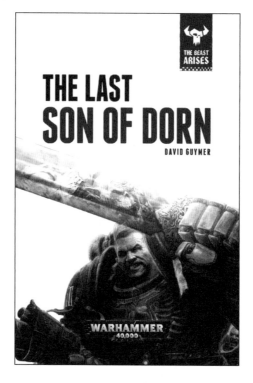

Available from
blacklibrary.com and

Extract from

The Last Son of Dorn

by David Guymer

Kjarvik Stormcrow stood in the the gunship's open hatch. One heavy boot was on the lowering assault ramp, the extended hydraulics gripped in one wolf-clawed gauntlet. The braid of heavy ork knucklebones strung through his long forelock drummed wildly on his shoulder. His pelt whipped about behind him. The unfamiliar salts of an alien ocean filled his nose and mouth. Before him was grey ocean, as far as his prodigiously enhanced senses and stupefying altitude could show it. Massive waves were capped with oily pollution and stuck through with scrap metal. It made them frothy and barbed, like watching the *hreindýr* herds on their winter exodus across the fjords.

The phosphorus burn of autofire tracers stitched across the streaking blue, the loose chain rattle of machine cannons barely audible above the roar of turbofans. The *Penitent Wrath* descended hard, hammered left. A propeller-driven biplane with a lightning bolt jagging down the side droned by on the right, and spat high-velocity slugs into the water.

Kjarvik held on, scowling. More of the atmosphere fighters were buzzing low over the ocean on an intercept course. They were not going to make it, of course.

The ork aircraft were remarkably capable given their ramshackle design, but they had not a scrap on the Thunderhawk's speed. And Atherias, the Hawk Lord, was good. Almost preternaturally good. His co-pilot was not too bad either.

The gunship bellied out, auto-fire crisscrossing the sky around them. Kjarvik beheld the mountainous structure that Atherias' evasive manoeuvres had brought into view.

Bohr would have called it an island hive, or the remains of one, but Bohr had no soul.

It was a titan of the ocean underworld, the burnt, bombed-out skeleton of a thing that could not die, its skin partially regenerated with drift metal, plastek sheeting and planks of wood, rearing up for the feast of metallics that glinted in the orbital band. Fat blimps and transorbitals buzzed around its thorny head like carrion birds.

Massive guy ropes held the teetering mountain upright, anchored within the sprawling pontoon shanties that crested and fell with the waves. The relentless wave action was converted into power by salt-corroded copper converters, fed into hab-size capacitors for storage or through fat cables towards immense desalination complexes. The dark blue liquid was slurped out of the ocean by the kilolitre, potable water and salts spat out into drums for export. Fleets of ramshackle paddleboats trawled the ocean for useable scrap.

Mere months after Plaeos had fallen, the orks had made their new conquest not just viable, but valuable.

'Twenty seconds,' came Atherias' voice, tinny in his ear bud.

An ork fighter came apart in a blizzard of outsize engine parts as *Penitent Wrath*'s lascannons neatly cut it out of the sky and set off its fuel tank. Debris spanked off the gunship's heavy hull armour, and Kjarvik ducked back to avoid a piece of propeller that came scything across like a circular saw and took a bite out of the foot of the ramp before bouncing clear.

He looked back out, saw the fighter's wingman pull a turn that would have torn a Lightning interceptor in half and spear out left. Machine-guided underwing hardpoints tracked it, mass-reactives spitting between its wobbling interwing struts as it flashed underneath the gunship, then pulled into a gravity-defying vertical corkscrew that swung the fighter-bomber in behind. Kjavik caught a glimpse of the pilot. Immense musculature, bulked out in furs and squeezed into a cockpit. A huge grin split the ork's ugly mouth beneath a set of red-lensed goggles as it mashed its firing toggles to send a stream of auto-fire gnawing through the Thunderhawk's blocky rear armour.

A ruptured oxygen main sprayed compressed gasses across the assault ramp as Kjarvik drew his bolt-pistol and loosed a flurry of rounds. The gas spray cut out as *Penitent Wrath*'s spirit redirected her outlets. The wind cleared the ramp, and Kjarvik was able to watch as the fighter veered off with a mass-reactive wound in her upper wing before breaking up in the water.

'Hah!' he roared. 'Did you see that?'

'A lucky shot,' Bohr chided, crackling in his ear.

'Better to be lucky than not, I say.'

'Ten seconds.'

The Thunderhawk's turbofans responded to the heightened strains of four armoured Space Marines moving towards its rear hatch with a barely audible whine of its already howling turbofans. Kjarvik looked over his shoulder.

Baldarich pressed Phareous' shield into his gauntlets. It was white against the fresh black of his armour and bore the emblem of a writhing snake. Phareous in turn tossed the Black Templar his broadsword. Behind them, Zarrael rammed the most vicious looking weapon Kjarvik had ever seen across his back. He called it an eviscerator. The Flesh Tearer was massive, despite the fact he had just knelt to strap a bandolier of grenades over his thigh plate. Kjarvik had seen orks smaller.

Kill-Team Umbra.

'Your helmet.' Iron Father Jurkim Bohr appeared from the cockpit hatch. Whipping mechadendrites performed final checks on his battleplate and moved, apparently guided by their own spirits, to pluck spare magazines and grenades from the equipment lockers. Other tendrils snaked through the cargo webbing, moving in a weird mirror-fashion to the stride of his armoured limbs. Two women in bulky pressure suits, back-mounted grav-harness and underwater rebreathers flanked him.

Despite their protective coverings, their relative stature, the women possessed a presence that engulfed them all, that the Thunderhawk itself could not contain. Ice was not so empty. They glided where the Iron Hand clumped, floated within a null singularity of their pariah physiology.

Kjarvik gave a pantherish snarl, and slid the black helmet over his mane as advised. It found the gorget softseals with a hiss of magnetic constrictors. It killed the wind, but it would take more than an environment seal to take the chill factor of the Sisters away. After a moment, his faceshield display came alive, pre-set with with counters clocking local probable and relativistic time. They were all blinking rapidly down towards zero.

'Five seconds.'

There was a time and a place for waiting. Kjarvik did not think that this was it. What was five seconds anyway?

He stepped backwards off the ramp.

The wind hit him hard and he began to fall. The thunder of turbofans and heavy bolters disappeared in the roar. He spread his arms and legs wide and let go a howl of joy. The black paint of the gunship disappeared. The wide grey of the ocean rushed up to meet him, waves reering up as though desperate to hit him before he hit them.

Then it did, like being rammed in the chest by a Razorback, and everything became black.

Eidolica – orbital
Check 7, -00:09:01

No one had ever called the Fists Exemplar homeworld beautiful.

Its sun was a ball of thermonuclear rage. The daylight terminator was a line of fire ten kilometres high and twenty thousand long, a creeping barrage of photons and ultraviolet rays. Barren mountains rose high into the atmosphere, what wind the world's torturous spin could generate insufficient to blunt them. Vast, black expanses of promethium sands covered about a third of the surface in lieu of liquid oceans.

From the Storm Eagle's open rear hatch Tyris could pick out the sprawling extraction and refinery complexes, a web of rust and piping and sporadic flare-offs that ate into the littoral boundary. A countdown timer hovered over his left eye, stretched slightly by the curve of his visor. He turned from the hatch and stepped aside. The deliberate heel-up, disengage, toe-down, and mag-lock gait came as second nature.

His own genetic proclivities, maybe, but the Raven Guard would always be more comfortable in the black.

'Nubis. Antares.'

The Salamander and Fist Exemplar of Kill-Team Stalker so named clumped up to the hatch. The sun burned a white stripe along the smooth relief of their helmets, pauldrons, and the lift jets of their jump packs. They stood either side of a third figure, similarly geared with a light-variant jump pack and grav-lines. She was tall for a human, but not so tall in the company she kept. Her ornate, high-collared armour appeared gold, but the thermal membrane that had been painted over the top dulled its shine. It stretched over her bald head and braided topknot like a taut skin. The infinite dark of her eyes were shielded by a set of flare goggles.

'Go,' Tyris voxed.

The two Space Marines pushed themselves through the hatch and into the thin, void-boundary layer of the upper atmosphere. The Sister followed a second behind.

'Next.'

Vega and Iaros stepped up to the breach, a second woman similarly positioned between them. If Tyris had once thought the mortal women in need of protection, then that misconception had been cleansed from him over the weeks of joint exercises and training. She was simply too valuable to go in first.

Mag-locked though they were, Tyris could picture the Doom Eagle shifting from foot to foot as he would in practice, eager to be away. He had come to know them all, better than many of his own gene-brothers, and he knew therefore that the Ultramarine would hesitate on the threshold and glance back.

'I have an ill-feeling about this, brother-sergeant,' said Iaros.

Tyris glanced to the silent Sister, felt his gut coil at the *nothing* that filled her space.

'Don't we all.'

'We do not,' voxed Vega.

'Go,' said Tyris, lest the Doom Eagle jump alone, and once again the three warriors push themselves through the open hatch.

Alone inside the coasting gunship's assault bay, Tyris moved to the edge.

He held a moment, hearts swelling, eyes drinking in the view.

There was no wind. No pull of air or *ding* of particulates hitting the fuselage. No howl of decompression. Just inside, outside, and nothing but the liminal between them. Half an eye on his visor's countdown timer, he spread his arms, disengaged mag-lock, and pitched forward.

Sunlight hit like a bolt round in the face. It overloaded his visor's antiglare and bleached his view to whites and greys. Bleeps and chimes alerted him to temperature and radiation warnings, failures in his suit's auspex, vox, and power distribution subsystems. There was a reason that Antares cursed with a reference to 'bright skies'. Work ceased. Cities were locked down. Even microbes could not exist on the planet's surface.

Which was why only a daylight raid would succeed.

There was no sensation of falling at all. The air was too thin to be felt. The planet was so far below him that the passing seconds brought its features no closer. He could almost reach out, and clasp a hemisphere in each gauntlet. If not for the madcap race of altimeter runes in his helmet display, he might have believed he flew. He could just about pick out the rest of his kill-team through the radiation glare. They were far below him, freefalling, but still in formation and descending fast.

He turned his head slightly and caught the Storm Eagle as it cushioned off the atmosphere and away. Twenty metres of inertialy propelled metal, unpowered, it might as well have been invisible. The precision calculation required to graze a body moving at one hundred and eighty thousand kilometres per second with another impelled towards it from a trillion kilometres away staggered him.

It could only have been achieved with the co-operation of the Adeptus Mechanicus.

He looked back to the planet. He scoured it for the co-ordinates of the Fists Exemplar fortress. Genhanced synapses lapped at the brink of the neural cascade that would trigger his jump pack as numerals raced across his faceshield display towards a string of zeroes.

It had to be all together or it might as well be not at all.

Soon.

But not yet.